THE LEATHER JACKET

The Leather Jacket

Stories by
Cesare Pavese

Translated by Alma Murch
Introduction by Margaret Crosland

QUARTET BOOKS
LONDON   MELBOURNE   NEW YORK

First published by Quartet Books Limited 1980
A member of the Namara Group
27 Goodge Street, London W1P 1FD

These stories have been selected by Margaret Crosland from
Summer Storm and *Festival Night* first published in hardcover
in Great Britain by Peter Owen Limited, London

ISBN 0 7043 3301 5

Printed and bound in Great Britain by
Hazell, Watson & Viney Ltd, Aylesbury

Contents

Introduction

Cesare Pavese, author of these stories, is now known all over the world as one of Italy's most important twentieth-century writers. He was born in 1908 near Turin in Piedmont, studied at the University of Turin and wrote an outstanding thesis about the American poet Walt Whitman. After working briefly as a teacher he began to contribute articles on U.S. literary topics, and also poems, to intellectual periodicals, soon becoming editor of *La Cultura* and a valued consultant for the newly established Turin publishing house of Einaudi. It was through his many translations that Italian readers were able to discover classics such as *Moby Dick* and modern authors such as Sinclair Lewis and Steinbeck. The study of writers like these helped to deepen his own concern for ordinary working people and also his insistence on realism, two of the most striking aspects of his work.

His own roots lay deep in the Piedmont countryside and he saw with sadness that too many of the people living there were forced to drift into the towns or even overseas in search of work. Pavese's sympathies lay with the left-wing thinkers and writers who inevitably opposed the policies of Mussolini's government in the early thirties. By 1935 he was one of the intellectuals arrested for anti-fascist activities and sent into preventive detention on the island of Brancaleone in Calabria. He was released the following year, the same year that his first book of poems appeared. From then onwards he wrote incessantly, using his personal experience and observation of life in both country and town, as well as his life in prison. His first novel, *The Beach*, appeared in 1942 and during the next eight years he published the other major books, including *The Moon and the Bonfire*, *The Devil in the Hills* and *Among Women Only*.

He continued with his translations, kept a secret diary, which has been published in Great Britain as *This Business of Living*, and wrote short stories. Strangely enough, he kept them almost as secret as the diary and rarely mentioned them either there or in the many letters he wrote to friends and colleagues. Yet the stories, nine of which have been selected for this collection, the first to be published in paperback in English, are in no way the minor works of a professional novelist. These taut, ironic, memorable tales in fact complement the novels with remarkable closeness, some of them obvious starting-points for the full-length novels themselves – *Land of Exile*, for instance, based on his own experiences on Brancaleone, was to develop into *The Political Prisoner*. And all of them throw light on Pavese's complex personality.

They reflect the three main areas of his experience – his first-hand knowledge of country life, which was usually far from idyllic, his sympathetic understanding of working people struggling to find some personal happiness, and his many disappointing experiences with women. His sympathy was for young, dissatisfied men, and for adolescent boys eager for experience of life, as in *First Love* and *The Leather Jacket*. Perhaps he remembered his own childhood, after the early loss of his father, and the years spent with his harsh, disciplinarian mother. As for women, Pavese wrote many heartfelt love poems but he apparently used his stories to express revenge on them; his women characters, whether wives, lovers, amateur or professional prostitutes, seem incapable of love and so, in reply as it were, the men in *Summer Storm* remain uninterested and unmoved when a girl is drowned in the river.

Pavese himself knew little happiness in life, and his journal reveals fifteen years of growing despair, a preoccupation with emotional and mental suffering from which suicide could be the only escape. In 1950 his novel *Among Women Only* won the important Strega prize in Italy, but even this success did not help him. After the American actress Constance Dowling deserted him he killed himself, with obvious premeditation, by taking an overdose of sleeping pills. One of his poems had been entitled *A Mania for Solitude*, a state of mind reflected by the man in the story *Wedding Trip:* 'I become so engrossed in solitude that it deadens all my sense of human relationships and makes me incapable of tolerating or responding to any tenderness'. Nature imitates art, but Pavese must have been aware that his characters experienced much of his own unhappiness. The short stories, all straightforward narratives in themselves, full of action and interaction, express alienation, a detached emotional and physical intensity which appeared only intermittently in Pavese's own life: until the bitter self-murder with which he ended it.

Margaret Crosland, 1980

Festival Night

Over the threshing floor, smooth and firm as a marble table, the evening air was rising, fresh and cool. When the setting sun has only just dropped behind the brow of a hill, the earth around the base of it seems to glow with a light of its own, a clear, serene radiance emanating from the stones and the bare soil. In the still air behind the cowshed, snatches of dance music could be heard, borne by the wind and broken by the distant hills, as if shrill voices were quarrelling far away.

Two boys with bundles of leafy branches were sweeping the threshing floor, their bare feet shuffling over its cold, hard surface. Darting sly, sidelong glances at the Padre, they seized their chance at a moment when he leaned inside a barrel and boxed each other's ears. A third boy, also barefoot, wearing long trousers, was sitting on a low wall, tying up his own bunch of leafy twigs with a strip of willow bark. Every now and then his hair fell over his face and he tossed his head to shake it out of his eyes. As the other two began squabbling he looked craftily at the Padre, who, with his cassock well tucked up, was still bending into the barrel trying to retrieve his stick, and hissed to the smaller boy: ‘Soak him with that liquid manure.’

1

Another barrel stood open on the threshing floor and from that one, too, came a powerful stench, its pungency softened as it rose through the cool dusk. The boy lifted his bunch of twigs to dip it in this barrel, but let it fall from his hand as the Padre straightened up, red in the face, and began wiping his fingers on his sack apron. The boy ran away, crying: ' Padre! Rico's trying to mess me up, Padre.'

The Padre glared, then turned to the lad sitting on the wall. ' You're at the bottom of the trouble! You're the rock of offence!' he shouted at him, wiping the sweat from his forehead with the back of his hand and coming to a halt in the middle of the threshing floor. ' It's always you, Biscione. What are you doing, sitting there? You've already had your supper, I suppose? Your belly's swollen! We're all good at making manure, but mixing it means hard work. Get on with it! Clean this threshing floor! It will soon be dark.'

' The floor is ready,' said Biscione, without moving.

Along the path from the dung-heap came the schoolmaster with his coat over his shoulders, buckling the belt of his trousers. ' What nice fresh air there is here,' he murmured, walking close by the wall of the cowshed where the floor was not beaten so smoothly. He came and sat down on the little trough by the pump, a shallow basin filled with rubbish, and stretched out his legs, breathing through his nostrils, his eyes half shut.

' Look at all these ants! Just here!' cried the Padre, his face to the ground. ' Look out, Biscione! They're on their way to a festival, too! How they run! They seem to know the maize is coming. We shall spread it out for them.'

' Rest for a minute, Padre,' the schoolmaster broke in, filling his pipe, ' and listen to the music. It seems as if heaven itself is singing and the very wind making music tonight.'

2

Biscione was sparring with the other two by the pile of branches. The Padre turned and went over to the schoolmaster, between the barrels. 'It's a fine rough wind that has brought us this music,' he said, 'and you talk of heaven! Anyone who wants to find our boys should go there and look for them among the circus tents. Sideshows and animal cages, cages and sideshows! How many came to school today?'

'Two.'

'Fine! And the parents are even worse. They eat and drink, drink and dance. They might at least listen to the music. Yesterday I was passing through the square ... it was six o'clock in the afternoon ... and, would you believe it? ... I saw that woman ... that station-mistress ... and she's old enough to know better ... arm in arm with her father ... her own father, I tell you. They got into one of those dodgem cars and started going backwards and forwards, shrieking, bumping into the other cars, crashing against one another like animals. Imagine what goes on in those cars at night-time. One man, they told me, had his hand crushed between two machines.'

The schoolmaster, with a wry smile, was watching the smoke of his pipe, and beyond it, as though through a cloudy mirror, the two boys who were tying up branches. Biscione had disappeared.

'We mustn't judge, Padre. Not all unmarried people are penitents like us.'

'But you know yourself,' grumbled the Padre, digging a bit of tobacco out of his cassock and chewing it briskly – ' you hear the young people coming home all night long on the main road, staggering from one ditch to the next, so drunk they can hardly stand, spewing out all the foulness they know or don't know, kicking at our door as if it were

3

a tavern. And there's no shortage of women among them, either.'

' All it means is that when the September Feast of the Madonna comes round a fine procession will sprinkle holy water on your door, too.'

' That's all very well!' snorted the Padre. ' Those circus gypsies know when they're on to a good thing and they won't leave the valley all that quickly. With all due respect, they're like this dung we're getting ready. Once you put your hands in it, you never get rid of the smell of it.' And the Padre again began rubbing his fists on the sack hanging from his neck. They were huge brown fists, streaked with black in every crease, under the nails and around the wrists. They looked like wood or shrivelled meat. Below the edge of the sack protruded his bare feet, and those, too, were knotted, covered with earth and twisted like roots.

' This smell isn't bad,' said the schoolmaster mildly. ' It shouldn't be unpleasant first thing in the morning, spread between the furrows.'

' As long as it's cow-dung, I agree,' said the Padre. ' But this lot, here, makes your eyes run. So scalding and acid it's no use even as manure.'

The schoolmaster puffed away at his pipe. ' For me, this is a sign of the good and bad aspects of our condition. In our body there is a devilish element – ill will – that poisons even what we expel. The acidity is of the spirit – ' and he peered through the rank smoke at the Padre's fleshless face.

' Very likely!' the Padre answered. ' Nothing easier ... Biscione! Are the brooms ready? Where has that rascal gone?'

As Rico and the other boy came forward, waving long bunches of alder, Biscione hastily reappeared, hitching up his trousers. The Padre went over to meet him, looked hard at his face and seized him by the wrist. Biscione was almost as tall as he was, but slender and not so deeply tanned.

'You went off for a smoke, eh?' said the Padre, his face close to the boy's. 'Where did you get the money?' Without replying, Biscione tried to wrench his arm free, while with the other he pretended to be fastening his trousers. 'You've been smoking,' the Padre repeated, without letting go of him. 'No nonsense! I can smell your breath. Where did you get the money?' Biscione did not answer.

'He'll collect fag-ends,' said the schoolmaster, from the pump.

'Fag-ends, indeed! I've even found fag-ends he's dropped,' snarled the Padre. 'He goes round selling baskets of peaches for me; if he doesn't do worse. Do you know you're stealing what belongs to the Lord? D'you know that?' Panting, he ransacked the boy's pockets, twisting his arm. He found nothing. 'At sixteen! These are the poor little boys we take in for charity's sake. " Idiots," the Father Superior calls them. In the ordinary way they'd sleep in ditches and come to a bad end. You're a fool, you are! So am I, and the schoolmaster. You're sure to end in a ditch, if not worse. Vagabond!' and he punched him in the face. 'Just you try and give me the slip another night, to go to San Rocco!' He hit him again. 'You don't know what you're doing!' And with a kick from his bare foot he sent him staggering three yards away. 'Get a broom and work, Biscione. That name is just right for you.'

But Biscione, who had let himself fall to the ground, jumped up and was on the point of hurling himself at the Padre. He trembled visibly, raised his arm, gripped the skin of his flank through his clothes and leaned forward. The Padre, furious, stood ready and waiting; his cassock had dropped down to his heels again, at the back. Biscione spat at him, gave a roar, turned away his head, then the rest of his body, started to run and disappeared behind the cowshed.

The schoolmaster had risen to his feet and was waving his pipe in one hand.

The Padre stayed a moment open-mouthed, as if on the point of crying out, then gave a shrug and turned to the others. 'Are the brooms ready? Now for the barrel! Remember, the hangman's bell-ringers don't stop working even for the Ave Maria. Come on, you others.'

The schoolmaster turned to sit down. The limpid air, clear as glass, was beginning to darken, softening and isolating the sounds that all seemed fresher, sweeter, under the bowl of the sky. Beyond the mulberry trees rustling on the nearby slope the hills stood black and distant. The bursts of music were more frequent now, more ethereal, throbbing in the tranquil air, freeing themselves in the sky from the tumult, the excitement and the wine that gave them birth – a sound as pure, as remote from humanity as the voice of the wind.

Bare feet were shuffling on the pale, hard threshing floor. The two boys were stooping in front of the barrel, ready with their alder brooms. They no longer looked at one another and seemed intent on some game. The Padre planted himself behind the barrel, his legs wide apart in their light-coloured underpants, his arms spread out to clasp the top of it. Like a wrestler he heaved at the huge cask, rocking it to start the contents moving. 'Ready!' he hissed. The two boys waited, tense and still. Then he gently tipped the cask forward, directing its mouth between them, towards the threshing floor. For a moment he balanced it there, at an angle, then slowly, cautiously, let it slant a little more, his body going with it. Panting and grunting, he braced the weight of it with his arms, his spine, the back of his legs and his heels. Away from him and between the two boys the dark evil-smelling slime began flowing in a rush of foam, dropping and spreading like oil. The boys leapt back. ' Get at it, you two!' roared the Padre, straining every muscle. ' Get into it! Spread it!'

The two boys bent forward, busy with their brooms. Every time one of them fell, the frothy mass splashed in all directions. Their feet made splashes, too, as they struggled frantically at their task, raising their hissing brooms, then quickly lowering them again to avoid the drips, their eyes screwed up tightly, their noses turned aside, sometimes bumping into each other, deaf to all else and working as if possessed. ' Rogues!' yelled the Padre with all his strength. ' Good-for-nothings! That's enough! Let it flow. A bit more round the side. You should be able to use up the lot ... Get some at the side ... Gently, now ... Go along with it ... Ah!' He kept on spitting and clearing his throat, still bent over the cask, still gripping it tightly as, slowly, relentlessly, it poured out the mixture.

Some semi-solid, semi-liquid splashes from the stinking flood even reached as far as the schoolmaster. He felt his head swimming as the fumes stung his eyes and nostrils, the distant music rang in his ears, and a wild impulse seized him to shed his shoes and stockings, strip off his clothes and plunge into the heaving mass, leaping and shouting, his beard flying in the wind. But he didn't bat an eyelid, except for the tears that streamed from his enflamed eyes.

The two boys had already calmed down. In response to the Padre's voice they obediently took short, careful steps and with their long brooms, now unrecognisable, they bent over and slowly swept the bubbling mass to get rid of the froth, pushing it away from them as they moved forward, glancing at each other now and then. As the last dregs drained from the steaming cask the Padre let it fall to the ground and collapsed on top of it in a single, shape-less heap.

'This smell, Padre, goes to a man's head like new wine,' the schoolmaster remarked from the shadows where he sat spitting.

'We're all a bit responsible for it.'

2

Rico set the big lantern down on the window-sill and peered into the storeroom. The wide patches of shadow danced as the flame flickered, the whole room quivered like an earthquake in the ruddy glow, then the dangling bunches of garlic, last year's yellowing corn-cobs, piled up sacks of grain, all grew still again and could be vaguely seen for what they were.

'Here's where you sleep.'

Barefoot, the two boys went in across the floor of beaten earth, leaving the light by the window. 'The Padre said we were to wash,' Rico breathed in a whisper. 'I'm sleepy. I'd rather stick my feet out over the edge of the mattress.'

'If the Padre catches you, you'll see what happens. Look at what he did when Biscione started playing up today,' muttered Gosto, under his breath.

'You silly ass! Biscione does it all on purpose. What happened to him? Nothing. Biscione ran off and came to bed. That way he didn't do any more work. Every time Biscione manages to get himself kicked out, we stay and do the work by ourselves. He did the same thing when the garden had to be hoed. Afterwards the Padre forgave him, but meanwhile I did the hoeing. You were in the vineyard, that time.'

Rico shook the lantern to put it out. Its dying flare danced over the three mattresses lined up against the wall. The furthest one was torn, and on it lay Biscione, face downwards with his legs together, his chest bare, his pale arms crossed under his head. He had not moved, not even disturbed by Gosto's muttering or the rustling of the dried leaves of the mattresses. As the shadows gathered, Gosto made the gesture of throwing a stone at him, his mouth distorted in an ugly grimace.

'No!' whispered Rico, and as he spoke the storeroom was plunged into darkness. There came a deep breath or two as they stretched out, creaks and rustles from the mattresses, a grunt and a sigh. Then the outline of the wide open window came into view again, a vague shape in the shadowy gloom.

Through the window, in the chill night air, came the sound of music, now echoing in the distance, now very close at hand, clear, yet faint. It seemed to breathe with the wind, suddenly ceasing, then coming back again mixed with the noise of the grass-hoppers or drowned by a gay voice singing, who knows where. Then the voice died away in the night and the wave of sound was lost among the trees.

'Rico,' Gosto muttered, 'you stink. It makes me sick.'

'You're the one who stinks. I ran round the meadow to wash my feet in the dew.'

'That was no good, Rico. There wasn't any dew by that time.'

'The Padre will scold you tomorrow. You'll see. You're not Biscione, you know.'

'Tomorrow,' said Gosto, his voice muffled against the mattress, 'I'll ask the Padre to let me go bathing in the Piana. He said he'd let me, if I didn't run off on the sly. I know a little lake, cool as a well, where the girls go. Once I saw some of them there, wearing only their shifts. I'll tell

9

him we're taking the ashes to the rubbish dump, and then we can run to the girls' bathing pool. The Padre lets us go and wash after taking the ashes, so we can stay there as long as we like.'

' How did you manage to see the girls, Gosto? We aren't allowed to.'

' There are rushes growing on the sand by the river. You can get quite close without being seen. You ask the Padre, too. Then he'll let us. You need a good wash, too.'

' Don't be stupid, Gosto. The threshing floor's finished, now. Tomorrow we'll be bringing in the maize. Workmen are coming and we'll all be off to the fields before daybreak. A fine chance that he'll let us go tomorrow! We'll be carrying so many of those baskets that we'll be streaming with sweat inside our shirts. Even Biscione will have to work tomorrow.'

Gosto gave a deep sigh and turned over noisily. The storeroom was alive with tiny sounds, the creaking of wood, gnawing teeth, the flutter of wings. Biscione had not moved.

' Let's go another time, with Biscione,' Rico whispered. Then, after a silence, ' Do the girls always go there?'

' If Biscione comes, too, the Padre's sure to notice it. He was already playing up, today. He's capable of starting to talk to the girls, and then I shan't be able to go there again,' Gosto objected.

' What are the girls like? Can you see them?'

' No, because they keep their shifts on. But you can see their legs. The big ones have legs as white as butter.'

' Biscione saw one of them once with a man, when he went to tread grapes at the Rossi's place. He says they were lying together behind the bushes in the Pratone, towards evening. They were doing what dogs do. He heard the woman laughing.'

' When was that?'

' Last year, at the feast of the Rosary.'

' That was wrong of Biscione. Why didn't he tell the Padre? Are we the only ones who have to make confession?'

' Then the man went away and the woman saw Biscione. She told him people are allowed to embrace in the grass.' Rico's shrill, breathless little voice broke in a stifled snigger.

' Ugh!' replied Gosto, stuffing his mouth against the pillow.

' Biscione gave me a cigarette, once,' Rico went on softly.

' Did you smoke it?'

' Sure.' Again a distant surge of music echoed through the trees. Rico paused until it was drowned by the shrill piping of the crickets, then he repeated, more emphatically. ' Sure. And he told me the Padre doesn't get goitre, simply because he chews tobacco. Look at the schoolmaster: he smokes a pipe and he hasn't got goitre, like you. You ought to smoke, to cure it. I'm going to smoke, so that I shan't get it.'

' But Biscione has never had it.'

' Because he smokes, that's why. He told me that the Padre won't let us smoke, because then we'll both get goitre and no-one will give us work outside the village.'

' But what about women? They don't smoke, and hardly any of them have goitre.'

' It's not the same for women. Besides, once in the main road I saw one go by in a carriage that came from Canelli, and she was smoking.'

There was silence for a moment, then Gosto said, barely forming the words: ' You'll see. He won't get away tonight as he did on Sunday. If the Padre gets to know about it, he won't let him come back in. That's why he was cheeky to the Padre today.'

' Biscione gets out when he likes and he always comes

back,' Rico stoutly protested, ' even if you spy on him as you did on Sunday.'

' But he was going dancing.'

' Ass! D'you think they'd let him go in the dance hall, barefoot? Instead, he went to see the menagerie in the big tent. He says there are so many other things to see, but that's the best of all.'

' Really?'

' There's a woman dressed to look naked, in glittering tights. She waits by the door and calls the people in. Inside there's a lion leaping about in a cage, and the trainer who rattles a pitchfork along the bars to make him turn. He says the lion roars like thunder. Everybody goes to see him. Biscione couldn't go in because it costs ten *soldi*, but he says you can hear everything from outside, even the tamer talking to the lion and the woman when she dances. Even the straw smells fierce, quite different from ours. When the show was closing, Biscione had a chat with the lion-tamer. He says he was wearing top boots and leather arm-bands. He's a Hungarian and knows lions as if they were oxen. He went into a booth for a minute and threw four darts: every one of them hit the bulls-eye. Then, Biscione says, he laughed and talked with the girls in Hungarian, and the woman who looked naked came along in those tights to take him away, and he ran after her with his whip all the way to the caravan where they sleep.'

' Does the woman really wear only tights?' Gosto mumbled under his breath in the silence.

3

There came a louder burst of music and Biscione suddenly raised his head. In the deserted night, that drunken tumult was the only sound on the wind. He stayed still, his eyes wide open, and soon he could make out the vast walls, the vague shapes of implements, the sacks and the dangling bunches of vegetables. From the next mattress came Gosto's rapid breathing.

Cautiously, Biscione got up and climbed through the window. Outside, the night was clear and cold. He looked up between the star-filled trees to make sure the night was still young. He did not hear the crickets singing. He ran lightly across the courtyard to the little door of the Padre's house. As he ran, he kept one hand firmly pressed against the leg of his trousers.

At the door he looked around, bending his head and straining his ears. In the distance the noise of a crowd was caught by the wind, but the music had ceased. Nothing could be heard, not even the dripping of the pump. He could have wished for the sound of a drunkard in the street, the howl of a dog, anything: instead, the night seemed utterly empty, hostile, making Biscione's ears ring, as if waiting.

A cricket chirruped. Biscione loosened his belt and took out the bill-hook. He brandished it for a moment in the shadow of the wall. The great hooked blade was cold but the smooth horn handle, broken at the tip, was still warm from his trousers. With a laugh he drew it across his cheek and the chill of it made him shiver. Then, silently, he whipped it through the air at the full length of his arm. If the Padre had had a goitre, like Gosto, that blow would have sliced it off. Biscione remembered when he had cut a grass snake in two. What a stroke! And the two pieces went on wriggling. A snarl escaped him.

He pushed the little door. It was shut. 'Bastard! He doesn't trust anyone,' he whispered. He turned and ran to the window. This was open – wide open. Biscione leaned through it and listened. He could hear no sound from the darkness. The crickets were now in full chorus, but he heard nothing else. ' If the crickets don't wake him, no-one can, as long as they don't start shouting.' Out of the gloom came a faint creak – perhaps a piece of wood in the wind – and the bill-hook slipped from Biscione's hand. Before it reached the ground he caught it by a sudden convulsive effort, then he groaned. Jerking forward, he had hit his forehead on the window-sill. The whole world seemed to crash around him, the night, the stars, the blackness. He fell to his knees under the window, dazed, filled with a presentiment of evil, his breath coming quickly, his spirit cowed.

Nothing moved in the room. ' Oh Lord, grant that he hasn't heard me.' Then he stood up again, listening. He climbed over the sill.

His feet on the cold tiles, he went forward blindly, shutting his eyes to accustom them more quickly to the dark. Suddenly he stopped. Far away, a dog howled in the night. Gripping the bill-hook, he strained his eyes in the gloom. He turned back to the window. Now he could see the first tiles beneath the sill, a chair in the corner, the vague outline of a cupboard. He swung round again: now he could make out the pale shape of the bed. He held his breath and took another step forward. Light blazed out and flooded over him where he stood.

The Padre was sitting up in bed, his hair on end, one foot on the ground, glaring at him with wide-open eyes, his hand still on the light switch. His loose nightshirt was undone, showing his bony leg protruding from the thrown-back bedclothes and reaching for the tiled floor. He pointed his left hand at Biscione, who was hurriedly trying to stuff the bill-hook inside his trousers. ' Assassin! What do you want?'

Biscione was turning his head in every direction, looking for a way to cross the room, jump through the window and escape in the darkness. But he felt the cold steel slipping down his leg and twist itself round his feet.

'You won't get away,' shouted the Padre, jumping out of bed, his white shirt flapping round him, ' you'll never get away as long as I live. Where did you want to break in?' He was on him now, hitting him. Biscione twisted round, trying to bend down. 'Stay where you are! Stay there! Every night we have more thieves. What's the matter with your feet?' Biscione tried to throw himself on the ground, clenching his teeth and bellowing. But the Padre punched him aside, then bent to pick up the tool that had fallen free. 'You rogue! Going round with bill-hooks in the middle of the night! What were you meaning to do with it here? D'you fancy you're an expert already?'

'I wasn't going to burgle anybody,' whined Biscione, clutching the table where he had ended up, very out of breath.

'It's all the same. A bill-hook's for breaking in some- where or killing someone. There's no one for you to murder now. What did you want in here?'

They stared at each other, dazzled by the harsh light, the Padre suspicious, dishevelled, as if his shirt had been blown on him by the wind; Biscione breathless, limp as the trousers that were trailing on the ground. They stared with- out a word. Biscione's mouth twisted in a faint ironic sneer. The Padre even had hair growing in the hollow at the base of his throat.

The Padre's eyes flashed at that look. He shook all over, as if he had ague. He turned his head this way and that, lost in thought. Then with a scowl he raised his eyes, passed the bill-hook into his left hand and with his right made the sign of a great cross, finding himself in some difficulty as

he tried to put his hands together afterwards. Biscione
stood waiting, hanging his head.

'Don't move,' said the Padre quickly. He ran to the
window and looked out, then closed it. He went back to
the bed to find his underpants. 'Don't move,' he repeated,
threateningly. He laid the bill-hook down on the bedside
table, hastily dragged his pants on anyhow and then looked
around for his cassock. Swiftly he whipped it over his head,
emerging with his eyes still on Biscione. The lad had not
moved from the table but was now leaning on it watching
the Padre's every move, still with the same faint sneer.

'There's nothing to laugh at, you fool,' said the Padre
coming over to him, fully dressed. Biscione cringed aside
as if to avoid a blow.

'Now kneel down.'

Instead, Biscione straightened up with his hands on the
table, still staring at the Padre.

'Kneel!' roared the Padre, raising his fist. 'Down on
your knees, you madman! You could have died tonight!'

Biscione let himself slip to the floor, knocking his knees
on the tiles. He saw the Padre's knobbly feet, then, as he
glanced upwards, his furious eyes glaring down at him.

'I repent, O Lord my God ....'

'I repent, O Lord my God ....'

'of the dreadful thought I had ....'

'of the dreadful thought I had ....'

'against my benefactor ....'

'against my benefactor ....'

'and I thank Thee for having saved me ....'

'and I thank Thee for having saved me ....'

'in Thine infinite mercy ....'

'in Thine infinite mercy ....'

'from the death of the soul.'

'from the death of the soul.'

'Now make the sign of the Cross and repeat the act of contrition.'

Putting his hands together at his breast, Biscione bowed his head and began mumbling devoutly under his breath while the Padre stood over him with outstretched arm, repeating the prayer with him. At last, Biscione slowly raised his head and the Padre solemnly traced on his brow the sign of absolution.

'That's better,' he said with a deep sigh of relief. 'Let's hope you'll benefit from it. On Sunday I'll confess you again with the others. Understand? Then you'll make general confession and we shall see what you deserve. You are to recite five *paters, aves* and *glorias* each evening from now until Sunday.'

Biscione had risen and stood tapping his arms with his crossed hands, looking doubtfully at the Padre who was mopping his forehead.

'Vagabond, did you mean to break in here? Don't you know that even to think of it is a mortal sin? Let us thank the Lord for his goodness in saving me, and saving you, too. What on earth's got into you? I hardly recognise you! All because I stopped you smoking?'

Fidgeting restlessly, Biscione let him talk, his eyes growing obstinate as he stared at the covered window. Then he replied, 'On Sunday I shan't be here.'

'What?'

'I told you before, Padre. I'm going away.'

'Where do you want to go?'

'I'll find a job. Anyway, I'm not stopping here.'

'But where will you go, you vagabond? Think of what you've done, and will do! Is this how you repent, how you turn from evil? God can hear you, you wicked boy. If your Padre doesn't keep you, who d'you think will take you? D'you really want to die in a ditch? We begin harvesting

17

tomorrow morning, and you with mortal sin at your throat? Put it out of your mind, Biscione. There's no need for you to run away. As far as I'm concerned you are forgiven, but God calls you to give an account of yourself and change your way of living.'

' I'm going away because here we are no better than animals.'

' Animals? How?'

' Beasts of burden. Say what you like to Rico and Gosto, in front of anybody, but don't give me that stuff about being a fool and dying of hunger. With the schoolmaster there, too. I work like the others – more than the others – because I'm no fool; but when I've finished, I've finished. I want to relax like the schoolmaster and everybody else; and to smoke if I choose, or go for a walk in the country when my day's work is done, like all workers. I'm sorry about tonight and I won't do it again, but I won't be such a fool as to go on working for someone who doesn't pay me.'

' Biscione,' cried the Padre, ' you repented and you can still think of payment? Is this how you fear God? At your age?'

' I don't want to rob you of anything,' Biscione went on, ' and if I'm young, that's not my fault. I work like anyone else, in working hours, and I've just as much right to be paid.'

' But your food, a place to sleep, what you wear, isn't all that payment enough?'

' No! It's not enough! The day-labourers you employ get their food, too. You give them rough wine as well. We get none. It doesn't cost anything to sleep. And the trousers given us out of charity are worn-out before we get them. That's happened to Rico twice, and he's so short he can cut them off at the knees. No, I'm not satisfied.'

Slowly the Padre walked over and opened the window,

letting a soft breath of night air into the stifling heat of the room. The wavering square of light shone across the courtyard and out into the night. There came from the darkness a confused noise of horse-play and far-off shrieks of laughter.

'Listen, Biscione. You were born in shame; you have no family, no-one. You came from the foundling hospital. It's no good thinking of the schoolmaster. You can't go to school, like gentlemen's sons. You've got a home here, you're learning a trade, there are good examples before your eyes. Why aren't you happy? Why don't you thank God? D'you think you could find work anywhere else, at your age, without our help? Shame is what you'd find, vices and temptations. You've shown what you're capable of already tonight. You might threaten someone and be taken seriously, another time.'

'The world is full of people who threaten and are still respected. When a man gets a pay-packet, temptations don't bother him.'

'Look here, Biscione, to your shame you're not a fool, but even if you'd been born mad the Lord would still have loved you. For men who work in the country it is a good thing to be simple in spirit and never look further than your own cattle, thanking the Lord for that much luck . . . .'

'You're no fool, either, Padre. There are other jobs, away from the land.'

The Padre came closer, his eyes sharp. 'What other jobs?'

'There's a man from the Piena earning four *lire* a day, looking after the horses at the circus in the square. He just gives them a little chaff night and morning, and takes them to the pond. It's already settled. I'm going to Alba with them.'

'Behold the Devil!' roared the Padre, starting back.

' Circus horses, running round and round all day! Going off to Alba! Living like a gipsy! To think of it! And that's where I came from ... They're always on holiday, and what are the consequences? Did they talk you into it? You're a penitent, like me. You repented. Vagabond! You dare to talk of payment? A man gets paid for working, not for going round the streets with music and dancing. Let that suffice! What other miracles did they lead you to expect?'

' You're the one for miracles, Padre. Who mentioned music and dancing?'

' Wretch! Vagabond! Don't you know they're all run-aways, delinquents? If you're already so wicked, with the life you lead here, what will you become with people like that?'

The Padre was thoroughly excited, waving his arms and raising his voice above a din that burst out at that moment beyond the trees by the roadside, an uproar of voices shouting and dogs howling. Even Fido had started barking. He was tied by a running tether to a wire near the railings, and the wire hissed as he chased up and down. Instantly the Padre ran to the window and peered out. He muttered harshly for a moment, then turned back to Biscione, solemnly shaking his head.

' This is what that sort of life leads to,' he said in a lower tone, his voice bitter. ' Is this what you're so keen to do? You've got it in you, you have indeed. But take care. Crafty men can be cheated by craftier ones. You wouldn't be the first they've worked to death and thrown penniless into the street when the festival's over.'

' It's hard to get paid anywhere. That's why I'm only asking for a half-day off. Half-pay till the grape harvest, plus board and lodging. Because I'm young. When seed-time comes we'll go into it again. Free on Sundays, and allowed to go out when the work is not pressing.' Biscione was looking the Padre straight in the face, his hands stuck into his belt over his bare stomach.

The Padre said quickly: 'I'll give you Sunday if you don't draw your pay and take advantage of it at seed-time. However, first we shall hear what the Father Superior says.'

'Sunday without pay is like mass without wine. And the Superior is you. I'm too young to bother about profit. It means that I confess to you on Saturday.'

The Padre pulled at his knuckles. 'Now it's time to sleep, Biscione. We'll talk to the Superior about it. Night isn't the time to go into such things and I cannot . . . .'

'Night or day, what's the odds? It's enough that we've come to terms. It means I can get away. I'll come back at harvest time when you're short-handed and you've hired me by the day. To keep me out of temptation. Is that all right?'

Slowly the Padre went over to pick up the bill-hook from beside his bed, then returned to the table. 'Biscione, you filthy wretch, you deserve to have this round your head.' Holding it out to him, he went on: 'Go to bed, and put this back where it belongs.'

'Of course, Padre,' and he stuck the blade through his belt. Then he turned, looked around, and came back to the table with an air of decision. 'But this is a mass without wine, Padre.'

'What's that?'

Biscione grinned. 'Good bargains are made over a drink.' And he did not move.

'Vagabond of a vagabond!' snorted the Padre. 'At this hour! Don't you trust anyone, you of all people?' But he went to the cupboard and took out a bottle and a glass, then went back to the table and poured the dark wine.

21

'Pick it up. I'm taking mass tomorrow and it's past midnight.'

While Biscione sipped it, there came another outburst of shouting outside the window and such a din of stones thrown at the iron fence that even Fido's frenzied barking barely drowned it.

4

Seated at a little iron table, the schoolmaster listened to the dance music in the square as it worked up to its final thunderous climax, more vibrant and deafening than ever. The roar of the trombones drowned the shrill clarinets, the cymbals clashed in frenzy, the trumpets joined in a long-drawn-out, ear-splitting squeal. Then suddenly there was silence, except for a low-pitched vibration, as if the voice of the music, having soared to its peak, had sunk down to earth again, humming under its breath.

In the cool night air, mellowed by the fumes of wine, he watched the comings and goings of the customers. It was stifling in the large room and the noise was deafening. The thick curtain of smoke swirled as men shouted to one another, all of them streaming with sweat. Around the tables were groups of carters with their red woollen sashes; old men from the country, their hair over their eyes; flashily dressed young hooligans; all holding glasses, sucking up their drinks with wet lips, banging on the tables, yelling, surrounded by a litter of waste paper and puddles of wine. Outside it was festival night, by God!

In his seat beside the door, the schoolmaster was cooling himself by holding his hand round the little empty beer bottle, leaning against the wall with his usual saturnine smile. Steering a course between the backs of customers in the half-light came a rough looking barmaid, a tall, raw-boned woman with big hips. As she poured wine from bottles or flasks, her lips twisted contemptuously as if she found the wine, the festival and everything else thoroughly distasteful. Every time she straightened up her hips bounced, and the schoolmaster half-closed his eyes.

Outside the door, where a ruddy light was shed by a lamp hanging from the architrave, a brawl had started between two deep-voiced country bumpkins. They stood there, their laboured insults inaudible above the noise of trumpets, the cries and the interminable trampling of feet, panting like a pair of bullocks. Stubbornly they persisted for a while, undeterred by the uproar around them, until the barmaid went to the door and stormed at them to go somewhere else. There was a silence, except for a wild burst of trumpet music coming from who knows where, then the two yokels pushed the barmaid aside and staggered in, arm in arm, making for a table at the back of the room.

The barmaid stayed by the door for a moment, her hips only a couple of handbreadths away from the school-master's cheek, stretching her neck in the ruddy light, trying to pierce the distant gloom illuminated by swinging acety-lene flares. The schoolmaster leaned forwards, too, peering between her hips and the door jamb, until the maid turned to look at him with a frown, croaking ' Excuse me.'

' Let's have more air,' stammered the schoolmaster.

' There's plenty of air,' she retorted, darting away as someone called her.

As the night proceeded, the din outside grew less deafening. Only an occasional burst of music raised its head, enlivening the confusion for a moment before it died away. One by one the flares went out and the crowd thinned in the square. Here and there in the distance, along the roads to the hills, shouting broke out, wavering in the wind. In the big room there were fewer people, more smoke, more wine fumes and a shriller babble of voices.

The schoolmaster had lit his pipe, wedging it between his sound teeth, and with narrowed eyes was watching everything through the smoke of it. The barmaid had come to the other side of the door and was sitting looking out, one large hand resting on her jutting knees. Now and then she glanced uneasily at her ugly, worn-out shoes. Her face was set in lines of utter weariness.

There came a moment when she broke into a smile. Another woman had appeared in the doorway, clutching to her breast a dark cloak that reached the ground. She was blonde and she looked furious, upset. She hesitated on the threshold and smiled at the barmaid. 'Hullo, Adele,' she said.

Adele twisted her knees aside so that the other could pass between her and the table, to sit in the corner. 'It's over,' sighed the blonde, falling back against the wall with her eyes closed. 'I'm worn out! More tired than a horse.'

Adele gave a thin smile. 'And I'm not, I suppose?' she asked, barely moving her lips. Then she rose to go away but paused at the door, her eyes searching the space outside.

'There's no hurry, Adele. I don't even feel like a glass of milk, tonight. There's a stink everywhere tonight. What a fug, in here! How they shout! And they stink like animals. Those at least can't wash themselves.' As she stretched her legs under the table her rose-pink shoes came into view. The edge of her cloak fell open, revealing the pink tights that covered her body as far as her breasts. Glimpsed thus, with her cloak undone, she looked naked but it was a lifeless, artificial nakedness.

'Still waiting for that fellow, Adele?' she asked casually, staring into mid-air through the smoke.

Adele swung round. 'I wonder why it is that other times

he jumps down from his cart when his day's work is barely over and doesn't get to his feet again. He sits where you're sitting now. Even when I'm dying to get to bed he keeps me here eating and laughing till daybreak. He'd even have me dancing if I listened to him.'

The blonde listened, rubbing her lower lip against her teeth, her chin in the air. She looked resentful.

' . . . and when San Rocco comes round I don't set eyes on him again. Off he goes in his cart, the sot, calling at every pub in the valley and sleeping under the stars. As long as the festival is on and there's a bench to be had, he doesn't come here, not even to save his life. He'll go and drink anywhere else, but here, no! I? Wait for him? Not likely! But what I'd like to know is, wine's the same everywhere, isn't it? Why doesn't he come here? It would cost him less, too.'

' No man bothers about the cost when he's out to enjoy himself,' the blonde replied slowly, ' and they don't fancy the wine they get at home. They stay away till the morning and then they're not fit to be seen, coming back with a splitting head, whining and moaning. And we're fools enough to give them coffee.'

' I haven't married him yet, so I can't order him about,' retorted Adele, ' but if he comes in here tonight he'll get coffee! I'll bash him over the head with it, the vagabond! In ditches, when he should sleep here with me!' The other barely smiled. ' Believe me,' Adele went on, ' I'm sick of it! Still, perhaps he feels bashful, and that's why he does his drinking at a distance. Once married, he'll no longer be shy.'

The blonde had loosened her cloak and was fanning her thin cheeks with the edge of it. In that dull pink sheath, with her too-red lips pursed, her light hair lifting as she blew, she looked like a picture from a calendar. In every

25

group in the room, men were eyeing her, putting their heads together and passing remarks. The schoolmaster gazed in the opposite direction, still surreptitiously watching her and listening, discreetly swallowing his saliva.

'For me, it's San Rocco all the year round,' sighed the blonde. 'We're always in ditches or bumping along the roads in a rickety wagon that lets in the rain. At least that carter of yours goes off by himself and you wait for him in peace and comfort. You don't have to trail round after him day and night as I do, with no friends anywhere and no company but two great insolent beasts. All day long they foul themselves and eat, foul themselves and eat. They've got to be cleaned and they've got to be fed, otherwise they'd fall ill and then we shouldn't eat, either. He never thinks of anything but those animals of his. If it rains we must go out and cover up the cage; if we have no money we've got to find some for them; if I had a baby they'd eat that, too . . . .'

The schoolmaster didn't even blink. ' . . . yet I'd put up with it all if it wasn't for the stink,' she went on, breathlessly. 'For six years all I've smelt is that stink. And everywhere we go the people stink, too. Blaring music, deafening noise, drunks, people with their mouths wide open, yelling, drinking. If it's summer, they smell of sweat; in winter, they stink of the stable. Some nights I even smell it in bed. He brings it to me. The minute we're shut he rushes off to fill himself with wine and rub shoulders with the crowd. He has a fine time spending the night in ditches till the smell gets into his skin and he stinks worse than the lions . . . .'

Adele had jumped up and run to the door as the iron-rimmed wheels of a cart approached, and the blonde went on, turning to the schoolmaster: 'Some nights I can't understand how I manage to sleep with him. He'd just as soon sleep in the cage. But maybe now I stink, too. What am I in here for, anyway?' Her eyes widened as she looked around. ' Wine and sweat. Nothing but drunkards. Give me that milk, Adele, I stink too, I stink.'

The schoolmaster knocked out his pipe in the hollow of his hand and mopped his forehead without answering. Adele turned from the door looking dazed, and said to the blonde: ' He's gone past!' Her breath came in a shuddering sigh.

' Who? Oh! Your carter. So you see!'

' There were four of them whipping the horse. Drunk already, and on their way to drink somewhere else.' The blonde took her hand as it lay clenched on the table and said to her calmly: ' Cheer up, Adele. The man I'm married to even left me stuck with the lions this evening, half-way through the show. I had to whip them through their turn myself. I'm furious about it. I felt as if I was beating him and getting my own back for all this filth. Who knows what state he'll be in when he comes back to me in the morning! You women in this part of the country never wash yourselves. Go on, Adele. Get me some milk.'

As Adele sullenly walked away, the schoolmaster cleared his throat and remarked, out of the blue: ' Aren't you hot in those tights?'

The blonde winked at him, opened her cloak and looked down at her breast. ' You want me to go without them?' she replied.

There was a brief silence, then the schoolmaster went on: ' I don't consider that you smell.'

' What d'you know about it?' said the blonde. When Adele came back with the beaker, she asked her sleepily: ' Has this gentleman laid his hands on you?'

Adele looked shocked. The schoolmaster's eyes widened and his mouth dropped open, showing his teeth like a horse. ' That gentleman there?' she answered. ' Why, that's the schoolmaster. He lives with the priest.'

The blonde opened her eyes as she drank, covering her faint smile with the beaker. ' I just wanted to be sure of it,' she said gravely, when she had finished. Then she pulled her cloak around her shoulders and went on: ' If you really want to, sir, let's go where it's cooler. These tights certainly keep me very hot.'

5

The Padre turned off the light and went out into the dark courtyard. Under the trees that hid the street he heard Fido whining, then the vibration of the wire as the animal bumped its head against it. He breathed the dog's name and it shot over to him like a dusky catapult, putting its paws on his stomach and wagging its tail. ' Good Fido,' whispered the Padre. ' The devil's even got into you, tonight. Good dog. On nights like this you should stay at home.' Fido rubbed against his hand, then stretched out its neck frantically whining to be let loose. The Padre pushed down the paws and moved back. ' Good dog,' he said again. ' Keep guard and set a good example.' Fido did his best to follow the retreating shadow, straining at the leash, half strangled; then falling back, struggling to get free and giving vent to a few muffled barks.

The Padre went to the storeroom window and groped for the lantern. He set it on the ground, bent down to light it, then straightened up, holding it at arm's length, suddenly casting its beam into the room and on to the mattresses. The great shadows loomed up and a smell of hay, sewage and sweat hit him full in the face. ' So they didn't wash, the little devils.' In the wavering light the half-naked bodies appeared, yellow and foreshortened. Rico was curled up, fast asleep with his face against the pillow and one elbow thrust out behind. Gosto, his trousers undone, lay on his back with his face to the ceiling, his mouth open, choking now and then from his swollen, brownish goitre as if it were a breast created to suffocate him. On the end pallet, Biscione lay at full length on his side, still in his trousers, his eyelids tightly screwed up against the light. ' That one sleeps soundly – just as I do myself,' the Padre muttered. For the first time he noticed that Biscione's cheeks showed patches of soft, reddish hair. Or perhaps it was the reflection of the light.

As he stood holding up the lantern, running his eyes over the sacks, the store of corn-cobs, the blades of scythes stacked in the corner, there reached him on the still night air the faint sound of a song from some far-away farm, a gay, deep voice that hardly broke the silence and softly died away in the distance. There, at least, was someone celebrating San Rocco on his own.

Bringing his mind back to the work in hand, the Padre lowered the great lantern and made his way towards the cowshed. Its low wall, white and unbroken, ran out at an angle from the side of the main farm buildings, under the hay-loft. The Padre turned the corner of it, lifted the lantern and pushed the smooth wood of the door. In the solemn darkness everything was quiet. Two oxen were lying comfortably on the straw beyond the ladder, chewing the cud. At the sudden influx of light they twitched their ears, still staring ahead into emptiness, their great muzzles undulating in response to the steady, silent rhythm of their jaws.

The Padre set down the lantern on the low window-sill. Beyond the grating, the circle of light shone over the smooth surface of the threshing floor, darkened and clotted here and there where the newly-spread manure was still damp. At the edge of it, the mulberry trees cast a line of dark shadow.

Pitchfork in hand, the Padre passed the ladder and slapped one of the bullocks on the back. The animal placidly turned his head, his chain jingling. The Padre prodded him with the pitchfork to make him rise. Puffing and blowing the bullock got to his knees, bumped his nose on the manger, then, with a wave of his tail, heaved himself up until his muddy great haunches were level. 'You filthy great beast,' said the Padre. 'You're covered in muck. Worse than the boys.' Planting his bare foot on the ladder, he drove the pitchfork into the sodden straw by the animal's hooves and hoisted up a large black mass of it. Controlling the handle with both hands, he walked over to the barrel at the back of the shed and shook the load into it with a sigh of relief. Then he brought back a forkful of fresh straw, threw it down and spread it under the bullock. Almost before he had finished, the animal dropped to its knees and settled down again, still chewing the cud. All this time the other bullock gazed into the void, chewing placidly.

In the suffocating heat, the Padre went over to the window, put out the lantern and stood looking out through the bars into the darkness. From the dark patches in the pasty mass on the threshing floor rose a stench not yet dispelled by the freshness of the night. Once it had soaked up the dew it could be spread on the land without a single crack, to soften and enrich the soil.

Still restless, the Padre cast a final glance at the faint outline of the bullocks, hardly distinguishable in the shadows, and went over to the big double door. Pulling away the beam that secured it, he slipped outside. He had just stepped forward to test the surface of the paste with his foot, when, by the uncertain starlight, he glimpsed a human figure coming down the sloping side of the dunghill towards the path. 'Who's there?' he exclaimed.

After a moment's silence, the vague shadow replied: 'Nothing to worry about. It's only me.' Jumping down to the threshing floor, trampling over the soft manure before the Padre had time to shout: 'Careful! Watch how you go!' the schoolmaster came across and stood beside him.

'It doesn't matter,' he cried shuffling his feet. 'Mud, dung and dew are the elements of night.'

'It does matter,' the Padre protested. 'You're spoiling what we've prepared with your shoes. Is this a time to be wandering about? I thought you were asleep long ago.'

The schoolmaster looked all around him, breathing through his nose. He raised his face to the dark sky, breathing noisily again. He watched the dim outline of the Padre moving back towards the cowshed window. He heard him strike a match, and in the sudden gleam of it saw him going to the threshing floor, protecting the flickering flame with one hand and holding up his cassock with the other, testing the state of the surface with his bare foot.

'And you? Is it night or morning with you, Padre?' the schoolmaster enquired jauntily, his voice vibrant with good humour.

'You, it seems to me, have been making a night of it' came the grudging reply. The feeble light flickered out and darkness closed around them again, blacker than ever. 'Haven't you been to bed?' the Padre enquired, breathing heavily.

'Too much noise, with all those drunks and festivities; even the crickets were too loud; it was too hot, anyway,' the schoolmaster answered boisterously. 'By the way,' he went on, 'I hadn't noticed that the crickets have stopped and it's almost chilly now. Who'd have thought it!'

'And it's nearly dawn already,' the Padre chimed in.

'Is it possible? How quickly summer nights pass!'

'Especially at San Rocco. The work-people will say the

same when they fall asleep in the furrows tomorrow morning.'

' As for me, I'm not sleepy, but I'm very hungry. I fancy I've discovered that night sharpens all our senses.'

' As to that, it's usual to sleep at night.'

' That's a pity, Padre.'

By now they could both make out the vague shapes of things in the darkness.

As they leaned against the rough stones of the cowshed, the low expanse of the threshing floor lay before them, shadowed on the far side by the wall of the first field, its slopes crowned by black mulberry trees. Beyond the trees, the great jutting hill revealed itself only as a space devoid of stars, a stretch of empty sky. A little eddy of wind whipped up the harsh smell of the night, and set the leaves of the mulberry trees rustling obediently.

' I'll sit here,' said the schoolmaster, ' and wait for the dawn.' He stuffed his pipe in his mouth and leaned back against the pump. ' It can't be all that long, now.'

The Padre was walking backwards and forwards over the threshing floor, intent on testing with his bare feet the persistent dampness of certain patches. ' If the morning sun gets on these puddles,' he muttered between his teeth, ' the surface will crack like glass. Damn those boys! Instead of spreading it out evenly they left lumps in it.' He licked his dirty finger and spat quickly before holding it in the air to test the breeze.

' How peaceful it is tonight,' the schoolmaster remarked through the smoke. ' Don't complain, Padre.'

' That cursed Biscione.'

' Padre, you're always up at dawn. Why have you never told me how beautiful are these hours of night? So mysterious, so tranquil. It's another world. Everything looks different, living a secret life. The strangest things

32

happen at night. It's a pleasure even to breathe, to be caressed by the darkness, the smells, the silence. One feels a bigger man, for good or evil. It's good to be alone, good to have company. Even this stink is good. It's fresh and warm, it's cheerful, it's human. To think that crimes are committed at night! How stupid the world is! Anything can happen at night.'

' Didn't you know that?'

' All I remember now is what I knew as a boy. But then I was afraid of the dark.'

' Listen, schoolmaster,' said the Padre, planting himself in the middle of the threshing floor. ' It seems to me that the fresh air has gone to your head like wine. Till yesterday I thought you an abstemious man.'

The schoolmaster bent over his pipe for a moment, then laughed hoarsely. ' As a matter of fact,' he muttered, clearing his throat, ' I have been drinking wine; the wine one can drink only at night, the wine of meditation . . .' He glanced at the other and suddenly went on: ' I'm happy to be alive, Padre.' Looking up again and waving his pipe, he added: ' Have you ever known this happiness?'

' Not on the feast of San Rocco, of all days in the year, and if you asked my opinion, I shouldn't advise you to look for peace and quiet on this particular night. Where the devil did you find them?'

The schoolmaster spat on the ground. ' I didn't look for them. They came to me,' he said slowly, with conviction, and over his face, already flushed in the mist, there passed a smile of pride.

The Padre shrugged his shoulders, then turned his head anxiously to the hill, now standing out black against the pale sky, and sniffed the wind again.

(March 5th – 29th, 1937)

33

Land of Exile

When a sudden, unexpected turn of events in my job drove me down to the far south of Italy, I felt very much on my own. The squalid village seemed to me a kind of penance – such as we each have to suffer at least once in a lifetime – and also as a place where I could withdraw from the world to sort out my ideas and find fresh experiences. And a penance it certainly was, all the months I stayed there; as for my anticipation of novelty and excitement, that fancy had me properly fooled. Being a native of Piedmont, I took such a jaundiced view of things down there that their probable significance escaped me. Yet I still remember it all – the little donkeys, the pitchers on the window-sills, the many-coloured sauces, the shrieks of the ugly old hags and the beggars – so vividly, so strangely, that I am truly sorry I did not take a more sympathetic interest in them at the time. And when I reflect how intensely I longed for the skies and the streets of Piedmont – where I am living so restlessly now – I can only conclude we are made that way. Only when a thing has passed, or changed, or vanished, can we really see what it is like.

The sea was there – a remote, colourless sea. Even today, whenever I feel depressed, I hear the surge of it in the back of my mind. On its bare, low beaches, every trace of land ended in a vague immensity. There were days when I sat on the shingle and stared apprehensively out to sea at the heavy clouds piling up on the skyline. I could have wished the whole world was empty beyond that harsh, inhuman shore.

The beach was desolate but not unpleasant. I was glad enough – since the country around was so uninteresting – to walk along it in the morning, or towards evening, keeping to the pebble ridge so as not to tire myself in the sand. I forced myself to take an interest in the little clumps of flowering geranium and the strong, fleshy leaves of the aloes. It always distressed me to come across a sandy shoot uprooted or crushed, the green pulp of its leaves all shrivelled up, showing the network of veins.

I remember one July morning when the heat was so intense that I could not make out where the sea ended and the sky began. A few yards above the line of shingle lay a cluster of shabby, weather-beaten old boats, one of them turned on its side as if resting after the night's fishing. The waves at the water's edge showed scarcely a ripple, as though they were cowed by the vast expanse of ocean.

Sitting against a boat in the shade I saw the convict from the open prison, a working man. He was gazing at the hill on whose summit stood the rocky white walls of an old fortress – the ancient village. He seemed fascinated by the limpid light in the sky that threw a bright veil over everything. He did not turn as I went by. He was wearing a peaked cap pulled down over his eyes and a brown suit, threadbare at the elbows and baggy at the knees. After I had gone past I heard him call me. A Turin newspaper was sticking out of my pocket in plain view.

While the young fellow was reading it, I squatted down in the shade of the boat to get my breath back. There was a smell of wood baking in the sun and of burning sand.

After a while I asked him: ' Going bathing?'

' All the papers say the same things,' he replied, fumbling in his pocket. ' Got anything to smoke?'

I gave him a cigarette and began undressing in the sunshine.

' I'm no politician,' he went on. ' What I want from the papers isn't politics. I like to read about what's happening at home. Instead of that, all they can talk about is politics.'

' I thought you might be . . . .'

' I'm a communist,' he interrupted me. ' I had a fight with a soldier, but that was a personal matter. I am a communist,' and he pulled his cap down over his eyes.

I slipped into my bathing trunks and sat down in the sun. I looked towards the calm, quivering sea, savouring in anticipation the foam on my face as I swam, the cool freshness of deep water, the marbled look of the sun below the surface. I felt very conscious of that heavily clad body still lying under the boat, almost out of sight. Long sleeves, thick trousers, rough cloth cap. The man must be suffocating!

' Coming for a swim?' I asked again.

' I'd rather have river water,' he replied, lost in thought.

' There's none of that here,' I told him.

I came up the shore, dripping wet, and threw myself down on the sand with my eyes shut. When I opened them again and sat up, I glanced casually at the hillside. The sun was still beating down, giving a red glow to the drab dejection of the thick plants and the nearby houses. My clothes made a dark patch beside the boat.

' And are you a prisoner, too?' the fellow called from where he lay.

' We all are, here, more or less,' I shouted. ' The only escape is to go in the water.'

' And what relief is that, in winter time?'

'In winter we dream of the place we came from.'

'I dream of it even in summer.'

He came over and sat down beside me on the sand. He had taken off his jacket and was wearing a dark sleeveless shirt.

'And the people who live here,' he asked, 'what place do you think they dream about?'

'They think about Northern Italy even more than we do.'

'Yes, but this is their own land. They aren't missing anything.'

Across the railway, between the beach and the first outlying houses of the village, came a group of women going to their own bathing-place among the rocks further up the coast; old women, heavily built and dressed in brown, but with them was a girl in white.

For something to say, I remarked, 'Swimming in the Po is nicer, of course. There's not so much sun and it's more convenient.'

'Where did you live in Turin?'

I told him.

'What are you doing in this part of the country, then?'

'I'm working on the new road. I'm an engineer.'

The convict wiped his nose against the back of his hand. 'I was a mechanic,' he said giving me a look. 'D'you get any mail from Turin?'

'Now and then.'

'I had some the other day,' and he dug out of his pocket a postcard with a view of the station. 'D'you know where this is?'

I looked at the picture for a moment, smiling, then gave it back to him, feeling embarrassed as I caught sight of the message.

' My girl sent it to me. The only time she writes to me is when she's fooling around with some other man. I know her.'

I didn't like his tone – he sounded truculent – so I lit a cigarette without answering him. I waited for him to continue, but he said no more. After a minute or two he handed me back my paper with a brusque word of thanks and walked away, stumbling through the sand.

2

Some evenings, on my way home from work, I came through the countryside bordering the coast, and, every time I did so, one thing struck me as incomprehensible. When a native of these parts has gone out into the world, how can he possibly think of this region as the one place on earth that means home to him, how can he feel proud to identify himself with it, regard it as life's haven? I was not thinking so much of the shortage of good fields and fresh water. the deceptive whimsicality of the thick stunted bushes or the bleak coast. Those things are merely natural features, and I myself was helping to modernise the, place by building a good tarred road.

The very life of the people was harsh and empty, their speech and customs boorish and uncouth, warped by race-memories from the far-distant past. At any time of day, the men emerge from their wretched hovels and casually saunter off to the barber's as if they had nothing else to do. They never seem to take the day's work seriously. They spend their time in the streets or sitting gossiping on their doorsteps in a dialect that, in the far-off mountains of the interior, is used only by farm-hands or colliers. Perhaps they work at night, or hidden away in their close-shut,

stifling little houses, but out of doors, from dawn to dusk,
they behave like idle tourists with nothing to do but enjoy
their leisure. And not one of them will allow his wife to be
seen in the streets. Old women can go out, so can the
children, but wives, women in the flower of their beauty,
must stay out of sight.

In this respect, certainly, it was an unfriendly place.
Even the men seemed aloof, not identifying themselves with
the village or their street, as if they did not belong there.
They seemed to lack roots, and their persistent vivacity
betrayed a physical uneasiness.

Still, as dusk fell, even the village grew sweeter under the
sky. A breath of air blew in from the sea and the half-
naked children played in the streets, while the old women
chattered in their shrill voices. From the open doors came
a stench of frying. I would sit outside a tavern facing the
deserted station, watching the herd of goats that supplied
the district with milk as they made their way to their stable,
or just drowsing in the twilight, enjoying the solitude.
Sometimes I thought uneasily that somewhere beyond the
mountains behind me, life in the great world was going on
as usual, and one day soon I should have to find my place
in it again. Someone was waiting for me there, and this
certainly gave me a tacit detachment from everything
around me, so that my very boredom encouraged me to
indulge in day-dreams. I lit a cigarette.

Suddenly Ciccio appeared from nowhere. ' Got anything
to give me, sir?' Rubbing his hands together in anticipation,
he added: ' I'm a smoker, too. Thanks. Your servant.'

Ciccio was a little man, burned brown by the sun, with
crafty eyes and a thin, straggling, grey beard. He was
swathed in a dingy cloak and his feet were wrapped in rags
secured with strips of leather. Whatever alms he was given
he spent on wine, and then kept out of sight so as not to

make a spectacle of himself. He came from somewhere inland and he had a prison record. The people here spoke of him with pride, as they did of everything else they felt belonged to them.

Ciccio was a half-wit, and every so often a fit would take him. Then he would rush wildly through the streets shouting abuse at various phantoms that haunted him personally. His wife had reduced him to this state by comparing him adversely with some other man. So Ciccio gave up everything – work, home, dignity – and roamed these coasts for a year, seeking he knew not what. Then he was put in a hospital, but he would have none of it and came back to the places he knew. So he became the Ciccio we know – the typical beggar who prefers a cigar stub or a good drink to a plate of thick soup.

Men playing cards in the tavern would drive him away, finding him a nuisance, but when they were idle and bored, or when there was a stranger about, Ciccio was worth his weight in gold – the perfect example of local eccentricity.

When he first started begging, he had been put in prison several times further up the coast, and this gave him such a horror of being shut up that even in winter he slept under bridges. ' Otherwise what should I have to put up with?' he once asked me all of a sudden, and I have often thought of his words. Perhaps he had been overcome by pangs of remorse that now gave a purpose to his life?

Though Ciccio was a half-wit, he was not stupid all the time. A breakdown such as his, suffering that turned his brain, could well have brought on his stroke, real or assumed, and robbed him of the right to complain. But in that case, deprived even of the comfort of railing against injustice, Ciccio would indeed have been wretched. At that time I preferred to believe he meant nothing by what he said – as begging too often makes a man do.

If people made vulgar or impertinent references to his misfortunes, Ciccio would reply with a jumbled explanation that changed the subject. When the blonde came from town, brought down in secret and accommodated for a couple of days in the slaughterhouse, the butcher himself remarked to Ciccio:: 'Look, Ciccio, you ought to murder that wife of yours. She's a whore now, you know, like this one.' But Ciccio, with a crafty look, said: 'If a woman goes wrong, the pleasure is hers and the sin is the man's – as far as we still know how to amuse ourselves . . . .'

3

At night, I used to make myself sleepy by sitting on the shore, listening to the wash of the sea in the darkness. Sometimes I stayed in the tavern studying the plans of the workings or glancing through my newspapers again, smoking and dreaming idly of the transfer that would have to come soon.

One evening, feeling restless, I turned away from the beach and was walking towards the country when I heard a voice call me. I swung round and managed to make out the workman from Turin, sitting on a bit of old wall. I was astounded, for I knew his rules forbade him to be out of doors at that hour. 'How are you, Otino?' I said.

He gave me a cigarette and we started strolling along the road flanked by olive trees. In the air was the pungent smell of September fields under a cold sky. The convict did not speak. We walked about fifty yards and back again, passing and re-passing the huts where he lived.

'This is a good way of staying at home and enjoying the fresh air at the same time,' I remarked at last.

The other remained silent. As far as I could see, his lips were tightly pressed together. He stared at the ground he walked upon.

' Is there much of your sentence still to run?'

Even this question brought no reply, but with a kind of effort, as though his throat was cut, he said without looking at me: ' I'm at my wits end about someone.'

I halted, took him by the arm. ' What the devil's happening?'

He broke away from me and stood still. ' I'm not telling you,' he muttered irritably, then went on: ' Women are rotten. Here I stay, living like a monk, and she just knocks around.'

' The one who sent the postcard? If you write to her . . . .'

The mechanic gave me a look of hatred. ' She was my wife.'

I stared back at him, aghast.

' When I was put inside she came to see me every day, crying and wanting to come with me. But how could she earn a living down here? There isn't a factory in the place. Then I understood and wrote telling her to come, but she didn't answer my letter. At this very minute she's in bed with some man or other.'

' But aren't you . . . .'

' We were always together . . .' He cleared his throat and I stared at the ground. ' Yes, of course,' I murmured vaguely.

We leaned on the wall where the mechanic had been sitting when I saw him first. The black fretwork of the olive trees made another wall around us. The man beside me took a shuddering breath as if he had broken a rib. Then he suddenly straightened up and said: ' Let's go on walking.' We started off again with great strides.

'But,' I began, after a while, 'the fact that she didn't write to you still doesn't mean that . . . .'

'Rubbish!' he cut me short. 'Not her. She's a bad lot. Even when I was there I never knew how to take her from one day to the next. She never let me know what was in the back of her mind. Not that she bossed me about, but she kept on and on. The only time I had any peace was when I saw her crying. For two years I kept her, and then she . . .' His words seemed torn from him against his will, and his clenched jaws made his face look even more gaunt.

'Why don't you write to her, Otino? Turin girls are kind-hearted. She'll willingly write back.'

'Not her. Six months ago I wrote, telling her to come at once. I've sent her three letters. You saw her reply.'

In his little furnished cell he went on talking. He explained to me that he was sent to prison because he tried to punch some sense into the head of a soldier who was having an affair with that wife of his. They gave him five years and he hadn't yet finished the first. He felt like battering his head against the wall.

'Why don't you petition for a reprieve?' I asked cautiously.

'A petition? I'll do that,' he replied, staring like a mad-man at the candle. 'Yes, that's what I'll do. I must . . . At this rate I'll get twenty years,' he added drily. 'If I come back.'

I looked at him uneasily. There was a worm-eaten table piled with crumpled newspapers, a filthy plate, and the lighted candle stuck in a bottle. Its light was dimmed by the stench from the bed, mingled with sweat and smoke.

He paced up and down while I watched him, seated on a stool. I knew the sort of man he was, surly and taciturn, and I couldn't think of anything else to say to him. At last

I ventured to ask: ' And you can't do without that girl any
longer?'

' I? Do without her?' he cried. ' I've done without her for
a year.'

He leaned against the wall. ' I can still do without her.
But for her to do without me . . . I don't want that. Now
you know . . . I'm speaking to you as a friend, even if we
aren't. If you've got a girl, get her in pod. It's the only way
to keep her.

' Calm down!'

4

All through the dull day, in that dull countryside the
thought of him remained with me – the obsession of that
prisoner tramping up and down his room or the beach,
seeking in vain for peace, always alone, staring in front of
him. He seldom let himself be seen – I remembered his
suffering – but to see him wave to me from a distance, or to
hear his name mentioned, was enough to make me aware,
with an unaccustomed sense of shock, that I was not alone
in that desolate region, and that someone was suffering
there as I could have suffered myself. That exile's fury of
resentment wounded me, filled me with a sense of remorse,
and robbed me of any further interest in the life I was
leading. Henceforth I longed to get away from it as from
a desert island. Yet, as the probable date of my transfer
grew nearer, I resigned myself more and more, with a sour
complacence, to the depressing atmosphere of the place.

Among the navvies working on my road were some who
had travelled the world without making any money – they
squandered it if they did. I used to find them at dawn, their
pockets empty, waiting on the doorstep of the hut we had

erected at the head of the bridge over the valley, already finished. I would smoke a cigarette with them in the chill air, as we stood drawing in damp mouthfuls with our backs to the low horizon of the sea. The navvies chattered away among themselves: ' At New Orleans I used to stay in bed in the mornings with a woman. There wasn't much work and life was easy. A curse on the season that drove me back to work like this.'

' Luck is luck. If you work you are swindled.'

' You ought to ask Vincenzo Catalano about that. He used to clean the keels of the steamers, and slept on the ground with the blacks.'

' No need to be such a fool as that. It's the country people that swindle you.'

' As long as you're with a crowd you're all right.'

' If you can get to Northern Italy, that's good enough.'

' As long as you're not a fool, anywhere's good enough.'

' There was an avenue of palm trees along the seashore, and once I walked along it from dawn to dusk without coming to the end of it. At night I was back in the city again, and it was behind that café that I met . . . .'

Now that the bridge was finished it was my job to act as watchman. All I had to do was to keep an eye on the three or four men who fired the boiler and planted pickets. Near the boiler was a scorched agave bush. The vapour from the tar combined with the brackish mist from the beach to veil the pale sun and sting one's eyes as it rose.

At such times I wandered away from the sea and up through the deserted street, looking up at those unknown mountains with half-shut eyes. In the street I sometimes met a peasant on his donkey, smaller than its master. The animal trotted placidly past me without glancing in my direction, while the peasant doffed his cap. He came from below those heights, a silent man from some thatched hovel or an ancient fortified hamlet, and scrutinised me for an instant with listless eyes. For such people the sea was a vague azure cloud. Sometimes a humble country-woman dressed in brown, sunburned and wrinkled, passed by barefoot, with a large basket on her head or a piglet tied by a rope, scrambling along on its three free legs. She never glanced in my direction, but always kept her eyes steadily fixed on the road ahead. I never had enough of these chance encounters. This was an unknown race, living its own life on its own land.

I returned to the hut and found the navvies sitting waiting for me, some difficulty having arisen that it was not their job to settle. So came mid-day, then the evening, then the morrow, and with October the heavy rains began.

It was impossible to lay asphalt any longer. The rain was like a waterfall. I wrote to the firm to pay me off and let me go; meanwhile I spent my days shut up indoors, in the tavern.

One day the butcher took me on one side. ' Engineer,' he said, ' put up ten *lire* and join a few of us. I'm writing on Sunday. The goods will arrive on Wednesday, and by Friday, any time you have a fancy for it you can knock three times on the door and find love waiting for you.'

The blonde slipped out of the train one wet and windy night, the butcher covered her with an umbrella, another man took her case, and they all disappeared in the dark alley behind the church.

The whole village knew about it, but at the tavern it was mentioned only between a few trusted friends. ' Keep it dark,' urged the butcher, ' and we might get hold of another client or two for Concetta.' They fed her on meat and olives, but they kept her shut up. As one man left her, the next went in. I was there the second evening. As I went through the dark shop I caught sight of two disembowelled

46

kids hanging from hooks over a tub. Then the butcher
came across to me, opened another worm-eaten door, took
me by the hand and led me in.

5

I often heard them discussing Concetta in the tavern. One
man called her stupid, another suggested sending her away
at once. The fact is that in the city, these girls are over-
worked. 'Next time we must get someone less tired.' They
were particularly struck by the contrast between her dark,
greasy skin and the exotic fineness of her fair hair. 'That
comes from mixed breeding,' the barber explained. 'She
was brought up at the foundling hospital. They're the best
sort. When I was in Algeria, I went with an Arab woman
as white as milk, with red hair. She said she was a sailor's
daughter.'

I swore to myself that I'd had all I could take. Those
discussions after love-making didn't please me much,
either. There's something degrading about listening to men
from another part of the world talking about women. To
change the subject, I enquired. 'Has anybody seen the
convict lately?'

'Sh!' hissed a young fellow, lowering his face to ours.
'Quiet! Not a word! Yesterday, someone from police headquarters came to question him. It was something about a
murder.'

'That gang of twisters!'

'Who was killed?'

'Nobody. They didn't take him away. They only wanted
to question him. It was about a crime that happened in
North Italy.'

'What do you know about it?'

47

'Nothing. I only know I saw him last night wandering on the beach like a man out of his mind. He had no cap and it was pouring with rain.'

I ran to look for him. He was not in his hut. I enquired of the neighbours. He had gone out at dawn, as usual. I went back along the beach and came across Ciccio under an upturned boat, binding up his feet. Ciccio had seen him. 'I'll show you where he is. Don't rush me.' We searched the whole village, No-one showed the slightest curiosity. Then we turned our backs on the sea and climbed the hillside. At midnight we came to a gateway in the fort, overlooking the roofs far below. At the foot of a column sat Otino, staring at the ground. He lifted a face ravaged by grief and pain and saluted me with a vague gesture.

'What's happened, Otino?'

'What was bound to happen.'

Ciccio, who had run to the other column and sat down, gestured to me that he wanted a smoke. I told him to go to hell.

'I know that someone from police headquarters...' I began.

'Everybody gets to know everything,' said Otino gloomily. Then he glanced round and noticed Ciccio.

'He's a fool. Anyway, he's not listening,' I said. 'If you want to tell me anything, go ahead.'

'Is he the one whose wife ran away? He must be a fool to let that bring him to such a state.'

'Otino, I've been looking for you for half an hour. They told me you were ill.'

'I?' He sprang to his feet. 'There's only one thing wrong with me, that sticks in my throat,' the words came slowly, one by one, from his pale lips. 'It's that now I can't do it myself.'

'Do what?' I murmured.

'But you know that,' he shouted in my face. 'You know it all. Why pretend you don't?'

'Otino,' I said, 'when I tell you a thing, you can believe me. I know that someone from the police came to question you, but what he told you, or what information he wanted, I have no idea.'

'Give me a smoke,' he said abruptly. I passed him a cigarette, then glanced at Ciccio and threw him one, which he caught in mid-air.

'Listen, then. My wife,' – and he tried to smile – 'my wife's been murdered by one of her workmates. She's lived with him for the past six months, but they'd been lovers for two years. Yours truly was questioned because " he used to frequent the victim – frequent! – and might be able to throw some light on important precedents".' Then, clutching me by the arm, he exclaimed: 'D'you know the best bit? He bashed her seven times, all in the face.'

He was no longer trying to smile. He spoke with a brittle lightness as though every word was forced from him, without raising his voice. When he had finished he sat there swinging his cap and staring at the cigarette, still unlit between his fingers. Then he started to his feet, crushed the cigarette in his fist and hurled it from him with a roar as if he could have thrown his hand as well. I felt the shock of it in my own arm, which he still gripped. Freeing myself, I said gently: 'Excuse me, Otino.'

'What sticks in my throat is that now I can't do it myself.' He gave another groan. 'Two years!' He took his cap in both hands. 'Two years!'

I turned away from that portico overlooking the sea, feeling callous and degraded. The two men who stayed there were not the sort to be good company. Yet I saw them a few days later in the square, sitting on a log. They were not talking, but anyway they were together.

I spent my last days wandering about, even in the rain. I avoided looking at the sea; it was dirty, turbulent, fearful. The village and the fields seemed suddenly smaller. It took me only a few steps to reach any part of the region and I returned unsatisfied. I could not endure it any longer. There was no colour left in the place. When the weather was bad, even the mountains disappeared – the background and the horizon of my earlier walks. The only thing still visible through the rain from the tavern window was the bare hill with the dirty-white fortress on its summit – the ancient village. This was the view that stayed in my mind's eye when, in the dazzling light of early morning, I moved on to follow my own destiny.

5th–24th July, 1936

Misogyny

The little tavern stood at a dark turn in the road, under the shadow of the mountains. The young landlord, Giusto, detested parties of trippers and would have preferred not to serve them, but this would have been unfair to his sister, who helped him run the place. Consequently his temper got worse and worse as the summer wore on.

One October evening when the place was deserted, the young fellow poured himself a glass of wine from a half-empty bottle, turned down the oil-lamp and sat with his feet on the table to glance through an old newspaper. He'd have been glad if one of his old customers had dropped in to liven things up for an hour or so.

'Mind you shut the door properly, if you're staying up,' his sister said with a sigh as she climbed listlessly up the stairs.

Giusto was left alone with his wine, staring at the paper, and thinking of his own affairs. There came a creak from behind the counter, where display-shelves with bottles of spirits stood in the shadows. Perhaps the wood was too old and rotten, or there was a rat about. No sound came from outside except a breath of night air through the half-closed window. Even the torrent that rippled noisily for most of the year was silent now. Summer was over, and all through the autumn the meadows would be filled with slow-moving mists. Indeed it was so quiet that you would have said you could hear the grass quivering or a pebble rolling down a slope. When in the end a cricket started chirping it made Giusto jump in his seat and pick up his glass.

'She's tired out, and so am I. Perhaps she's working too hard. If she married she'd have something to work for, but not even a carter will have her.'

Giusto moistened his lips again, then stopped as he heard footsteps in the courtyard and low voices. He recalled that a little while ago he had caught the sound of a car in the distance, and he raised his eyes. A human face was staring in at the window, someone said : 'Yes, yes,' hastily and the door opened.

Two young people, hand in hand, slipped inside; a thin, cautious-looking lad with broad shoulders and a dark-haired girl with big eyes, wearing a transparent mackintosh. They both halted just inside the door and stared at Giusto without speaking. The girl was carrying a suitcase and the boy, who looked at him, kept rubbing his forehead.

'Good evening,' Giusto greeted them.

The lad darted a glance at him and without coming forward asked bluntly if he could get any petrol there.

'Where's the car?' said Giusto.

The car had come to a halt on the main road. It had run out of petrol. They were in a hurry.

'I haven't any petrol,' Giusto answered placidly as he eyed the girl.

The lad turned pale and Giusto saw his eyes close for a moment. His face seemed bloodless under his bony forehead. As for the girl, she was sitting dejectedly on the suitcase, watching her companion's face as though her fate depended on him. 'Don't say anything, we'd better not say anything, Renato,' she hissed hurriedly. 'Who's to blame, anyway? Don't do anything, don't say anything. Where shall we go now, Renato?'

Giusto looked at the man again and saw that he had no idea what to do. He laughed and suggested they could spend the night at the inn.

'We can't do that,' the girl replied hastily. 'What about the car? We can't stay here.'

Giusto retorted crossly that they weren't the first to stay there. 'The car? We'll go and push it into the yard, I and the gentleman. Is it far away? Where d'you come from?'

They answered vaguely, Giusto persisted, and in the end they both admitted they were on their way to France. 'That's fine. In the morning we'll get the first cyclist who goes by to fetch a can from the village. Then you'll be all right. You can go where you like, but if you're going over the mountains take care you don't run dry again. You won't get any more up there.'

'Can't we go to the village ourselves, now?'

'I've already told you that's no good. The people who sell it are all fast asleep long ago.'

'Don't listen to him, Renato. Don't believe him. He's only trying to make us stay here. Let's go.'

By this time the boy had regained some self-control. He shut the door and came forward into the middle of the room. 'Tell me the real truth,' he said, 'and I'll pay double your charge for the night. Is there anywhere at all I can get petrol quickly?'

Giusto had an impulse to spit at his feet, but then realized the poor fellow was overwrought. The girl, too, huddled on the suitcase, seemed in a fever of agitation and never took her eyes from his back. He shook his head and called Tosca. Then he stood up and told them firmly: 'No petrol till tomorrow. Shall we go and get the car?'

The girl jumped up, thrust the suitcase against the wall with her foot and clutched her companion's arm, begging him not to leave her there alone. 'Here's my sister,' said

Giusto. 'She's coming down now,' and he drank up the rest of his wine.

All the time they were outside, walking in the dark between fields, Giusto never opened his mouth. They found the car, switched on the headlights and slowly, laboriously, began to push it. When the other ventured to say a word or two, Giusto made no answer except to mutter that they'd both better forget the girl.

When they arrived back, panting and sweating, they found the little room empty. The girl's little motoring hat lay on the floor beside the suitcase and Giusto picked it up. He went over to the foot of the stairs and heard the two women moving about overhead. 'Here we are,' he shouted.

'They're not answering,' the boy exclaimed a moment later. Giusto reassured him and asked if they'd like to go to bed now.

'Go to sleep?'

'I suppose so,' Giusto retorted impatiently. 'Naturally, if the young lady permits.'

'Poor girl,' said the other, his fleshless face twisted in a forced smile. 'Poor little thing. No, I'm not going to bed', and he ran his hand through his hair.

Giusto stepped over to the counter, picked up a bottle, filled a couple of little glasses and invited the boy to have a drink. 'Cognac,' he said, smacking his lips. The other swallowed it in one gulp with his eyes closed, then ran up the stairs.

II

Giusto went back to his seat at the table where he had tossed the paper. For a moment there was a buzzing in his ears, then all was silence except for an occasional footstep overhead. 'A dog,' he was thinking. 'That's what we want in this inn. People come and go without anybody knowing.' At that moment Tosca appeared, looking cross and pre-occupied. 'She's thrown herself down on the bed,' she snapped.

'And he hasn't?'

'He's just standing there licking his hand and looking on the floor.'

'They aren't married. She isn't wearing a wedding ring. But they don't look like kids running away from home.'

'She's thirty at least. Perhaps she's his sister.'

Giusto smiled scornfully. 'They're afraid of each other. He hardly dared go upstairs. And a man doesn't drive round at night with a nervous sister and forget about petrol.'

'They haven't had any supper,' Tosca replied.

'That's what I thought. They haven't even got any rugs in the car for crossing the mountain.'

'Hush.'

The boy appeared at the top of the stairs. With that pale face of his he looked like an invalid who had just crawled out of bed.

'Anything the matter?'

He came forward uncertainly. 'The case. Where's the suitcase?'

Giusto stood up. 'Nobody's taken it,' and he went towards the door to pick it up. 'I'll do that,' the boy cried as he ran forward. 'I'll get it.'

'No you won't,' said Giusto. 'That's my job. Yours is to fill in the register. Tosca, the register.'

He walked up the stairs, but the boy came beside him and took the case from his hand. 'Listen,' he said. 'The lady isn't well. Can you give us some milk?'

Tosca carried up the milk. She was very much put out

and remarked as she climbed the stairs : 'We shan't get any sleep tonight. The girl's feverish.'

'D'you think they've come here for her to have a baby?' Giusto piped up.

'Wretch !' his sister retorted. 'Go to bed ! Off to bed with you.'

At this rebuff Giusto wrinkled his nose with amusement and got ready to go up. 'We'll have a baby here tomorrow,' he laughed, outside the room where the two visitors were. 'Oh, well. As long as they don't leave it here,' and he went on to his own room.

A violent shake from Tosca woke him at dead of night. She was so weary she could hardly stand. How they'd kept her at their beck and call ! The woman had been delirious, thrown herself out of bed, wanted to go and get the car.

'And the baby?'

'What baby? They're scared to death, those two. They've done something. If you speak to them when they don't expect it they jump like rabbits.'

Giusto stammered something or other in the dark to reassure Tosca, and began to dress. It was cold. He wrapped his coat around him and went out on the landing, tip-toeing across to the crack of light from the other room. He heard a deep sigh and whispering voices. He shook his head and went on downstairs.

Once on the ground-floor he went across to the door and threw it open. The lamp still burned faintly but outside it was pitch dark. He could not see the sky. Chilled to the bone, he shut the door again and came over to the table to his old seat. The bottle was still there.

More than an hour went by as he dozed, woke with a start and moistened his lips now and then. That old newspaper was still before his eyes but he could not manage to read. At intervals a curl of smoke rose from the lamp.

He heard an uncertain footstep on the stairs and saw

a red pin-point light from a cigarette. 'Who's there?' he called.

The young man came forward, paler than ever, his eyes sunk in his head with weariness. He wanted a drink. Giusto went to fetch some cognac. 'Is the girl asleep?' he asked softly.

They sat facing one another in silence, each scrutinizing the other. The boy's two-day growth of beard made him look still more down and out. He drank at a draught, saying nothing.

'This warms the cockles of your heart,' Giusto told him. 'Takes away your palpitations. Women don't understand that.'

The other sat crouching forward and seemed to be listening. 'Doesn't anybody go past here at night?' he asked suddenly in a hoarse voice.

'Not very often,' Giusto replied. 'If they ever do it's in the summer, towards morning. Lorry drivers. Sometimes the customs officers.'

'Customs officers? Where do they go?'

'They just have a drink and then go on their rounds. But there aren't any law-breakers in these parts.'

The young man rose to his feet and began pacing up and down. Giusto followed him with his eyes.

'Is the frontier far from here?'

'Six hours by car. Anyone whose passport's in order finds it better to go by train.'

'We've got a passport,' the other broke in. 'It's just that we prefer . . .'

'To forget about petrol,' Giusto finished the sentence for him.

'You don't believe me?'

'My dear sir, it's my job to believe everybody. If an old man in a fur coat arrives in a car with a painted trollop and tells me she's his daughter, I must believe him. And if a couple come with no papers and suffering from insomnia, and the fellow is so scared he'd pay me anything to get away, I don't have to punch his nose. But I can tell him, however, man to man, that getting to the frontier is nothing. It's crossing it that's the problem, especially with a woman who can't keep quiet.'

The lad halted, his hands in his pockets. He lifted his right hand to his face and gnawed at it. He said in a low voice. 'If I've given you any trouble, please excuse me. There's nothing I can say. I cannot defend myself. All I want to do is sleep.'

He dropped into a chair, utterly exhausted. 'Take it from me, you won't have any trouble. You don't know us, and we'll leave at dawn.'

Giusto looked round in annoyance. He fancied he saw eyes shining in the passage at the top of the stairs. He restrained himself. 'And all this for a woman?' he asked, his voice expressionless. 'What have you done?'

The lad raised his pale face, his pupils flickering feverishly in their sockets under his bony forehead.

'What have you done?' Giusto asked once more.

III

'Are you sure the girl's asleep?' Giusto went on. 'All that agitation, that anxiety about getting away, that fear that leaves her breathless . . . can she possibly sleep with all that on her mind?'

'No,' said the boy, 'she's not asleep. It's as if she were drugged. She's not dreaming, but she sees things. She's seeing them all the time. We've spent two nights like this.

'What does she see?'

'What we're running away from.'

'Prison?'

'Oh,' said the boy in a whisper, 'if I were innocent, I'd
go to prison at once and stay there for years, all my life.
I wouldn't mind! I'd know they were doing me an injustice. But she'd have to go there, too. She who was
forced to do what she did, and in there nobody feels any
pity: there's no more justice or injustice. It's remorse that
prevents us from sleeping. She doesn't deserve it: she
was forced. And now she must endure injustice and terror.'

From the top of the stairs came a wild uncontrollable
cry: 'Renato! I'm all alone up here.'

The wretched youth started to his feet and stared wildly
at Giusto. 'Was she listening to us?' he exclaimed. 'My
head's splitting. I don't know what I was saying.'

'Go on up,' Giusto urged him. 'You're even more feverish
than she is. But have a drink first,' and he poured him
another cognac. His companion made some vague reply
and rushed up the stairs.

Soon every voice was silent. Giusto felt a need to sit
and think. The lamp, practically burnt out, flickered wearily
among the shadows. 'And that's the man who wants to get
into France,' Giusto murmured. 'How will they manage?
What will they do?'

He stretched out his hand to turn up the lamp and
watched it grow pale. A faint light was coming through
the windows. Now he could see the chairs and the calendar
on the door. The wind was whistling through the cracks.
Giusto's mouth felt dry so he picked up his glass, then
listlessly set it down again.

He woke to hear Tosca bustling about in her slippers.
She came out of the kitchen looking grey and untidy. The
lamp had gone out but it was now light enough to see.
'Did they call you in the night?' Her voice was hoarse and
she sounded surprised. Giusto cleared his throat and stood
up. 'I was asleep,' he said. 'It's bitterly cold.'

He went to the door and threw it open. In the damp, grey light he saw the low car close by, its windows misted over. 'If they're awake they'll need something to eat,' he said. 'I'm going over to the Grange, to get them to fetch a can of petrol.'

'Who's going to pay for it?' Tosca asked sharply.

It was drizzling with rain when he got back. He found the couple sitting at table and Tosca pouring out coffee. The boy swung round in wild alarm and Giusto winked at him. Then he looked at the girl. 'There'll be some petrol soon,' he told her. 'How have you slept?'

Her drawn cheeks managed to produce a defiant smile. 'Quite well,' she replied, looking up at him.

'I heard you were feverish. Cognac's the thing for that. You should try it. Your husband does.'

Those big eyes in her little face clouded over at his words. Restlessly the boy pushed away his cup. Giusto went on : 'My sister heard you raving in the night. Be careful once you're in France. Better stuff a handkerchief in your mouth.' Tosca stood stock-still in surprise. There came a scratching at the door.

In the silence an old man entered, muffled in an army greatcoat, scraping his feet along the floor. He greeted them all in a husky voice, putting a hand to his beret and giving them a little bow. They sat watching him as if hypnotized. His face was as wrinkled as a baby's.

'It's nothing,' Giusto broke in. 'Pedrotto just wants some milk.'

The old man shook the wet from him like a dog and went to the counter. Tosca ran over and poured him a drink. 'Pedrotto.' Giusto asked casually, 'Is there still a way across the frontier?'

The old fellow spluttered over his little glass and leered round at them. 'A clever man, on foot, can always get through,' he replied cautiously in a low voice.

'And a woman?'

'That depends.'

Giusto bent his head down between the couple. 'D'you want him?' he asked softly. 'Don't give him more than a hundred, and then only after he's finished the job. He'll go and wait for you on the road beyond the village. But watch out! He's much craftier than you are.'

Tosca had disappeared. 'My sister will pack you a picnic basket,' Giusto went on. 'You were even forgetting that petrol. Your trip may take time. You don't want to die of hunger on the way. But think it over carefully. Once you're in his hands there can be no turning back.'

The lad's indecision showed in his eyes, but the girl looked at Giusto and said firmly : 'All right.'

The old man went out and they all stood up. 'Don't bother about showing your passport.'

'We haven't got one,' she replied.

By now dawn had broken but a thick mist was drifting in through the half-open door. While Tosca and the girl were discussing the bill, Giusto went outside with the lad, who was biting his colourless lips. 'Be on your toes at the filling station,' Giusto advised him. 'Don't act as if you're desperate.' The lad nodded obediently and paid for the petrol.

Giusto slipped stealthily upstairs, fetched a blanket from the bed and tossed it into the car. 'It's up to you to look after her. Don't let her die of cold.' Leading his companion on one side, he told him : 'All this is nothing to do with me. I don't know what you may have done. But I'm thirty, and I've always noticed that women manage to get out of trouble, leaving the man in the soup. It just can't be helped.'

The boy gave him a twisted smile. 'And how much will the blanket cost us?' he asked.

'Nothing,' Giusto retorted and they went back inside.

The girl was waiting, sitting by the table. She had put on her hat and renewed her lipstick. Her face looked different, sharper than before and more lined. A deathly paleness made her eyes seem sunken and wisps of hair hung round her temples. Telling her companion to pay Tosca, she came to the door with the suitcase. Giusto stood aside to let her pass and then ran to open the car door for her. She jumped in.

The boy came up, and Tosca with the picnic basket. 'When you're among the snows, don't give Pedrotto anything to drink,' Giusto advised, leaning into the car. 'He's drunk enough already.'

The boy got in and switched on the engine. The car backed away, then turned into the road. 'Goodbye,' the girl cried.

'We shall always remember you,' said the boy, leaning out.

'They'd do better to forget all about us,' Giusto muttered to Tosca as she stood shivering in the fog.

The Cornfield

As long as the season was still young, no one paid any attention to those tender green shoots, though they were taller than usual, but as the hours of twilight lengthened and people strolled along the roads to enjoy the cool evening air, everyone noticed the growing corn. It would have grown still higher, yellow and rustling, with a poppy or two here and there, and one fine day the old man would have wanted to reap it, make it into sheaves and talk about it in the streets and the shops. Perhaps he would have tried to sell it.

Amalia noticed a group of lads crowding round the seat by the roadside, just where the factory wall ended and the strip of field began, in front of the house. She watched them anxiously. In a way she was ashamed of the corn, yet when it was green, as it was now, it gave her a surge of hope for something she could not have explained. But the lads only looked at it for a while, then went away.

One evening, while the factory workers who lived in the last houses before the boundary were cycling past, Amalia came home carrying her hat, holding her head high so as not to see the green stalks. She ate hastily, not noticing the broken crockery or the dirty litter strewn around the kitchen. She ate what there was; to her it was unimportant;

so were her mother's worn-out shoes and the old man's
unbuttoned trousers or the way he wiped his mouth on the
back of his hand. Her only concern was to be quick so that
she could get away and not have to listen to the old man
going on again about his corn and grumbling that the
manure had not fertilized it properly.

Still hatless, she went out into the dusk, hurrying away
from the house because she did not want Tosca to call for
her there. Humming to herself, she made her way to the
end of the road where the trees began again, and looked up
to see if there was a light in Tosca's apartment. The avenue
was full of children, playing and shrieking as long as there
was a scrap of daylight left. Amalia stopped by the mirror
at the American Bar to put on fresh lipstick and rearrange
her fringe of hair. In the greenish reflection her eyes looked
deep-set and cruel.

Tosca had once told her she envied their isolated hovel.
All Tosca had in mind was the convenience of not having
to do the stairs. For Tosca, Sunday was a grand day,
especially when she could go and picnic in the fields. Her
idea of bliss was to spend the whole day picking grapes.

Someone stared at her. It was Tosca's brother, Tonino.
Amalia had once told him plainly she disliked him. She
could not stand his ugly, pasty face and spiteful eyes or his
great dangling hands with their bitten nails. This time he
smiled and muttered something complimentary without
moving out of her way.

' Shall I go first, or will you?' she asked, infusing a little
sweetness into her answering smile.

' If you put it like that, I'll follow you,' Tonino replied,
holding out his hand.

' I'm waiting for Tosca.'

' I'm not,' he shrugged. Amalia stamped her foot impatiently, but Tonino laughed at her, looking pleased with

himself. Fuming, Amalia turned her back on him and sauntered away.

When she had left him behind she wandered up the avenue alone under the shade of the trees. Everywhere the stink of frying was blending with the dusty smell of the street, but through it all she could feel the cool evening breeze and it pleased her. The clatter of a tram in the distance pleased her, too.

Later in the evening, Amalia inspected the panels of photographs under the red lights outside the cinema and made a face. Tosca was not keen on going in, either, so they strolled around and eventually paused in front of the pleasure gardens called the *Giardino*.

'I'll see if there's anyone inside that we know,' Tosca said. A hand waved at them from a little group sitting just inside the fence. ' Come on!' Tosca cried. ' There's Gianni.'

' We haven't even got hats on,' Amalia protested.

' What odds? Some girls take them off, anyway. Come on!'

Gianni was there, so was Tonino, so were all the young factory workers in the district, drinking beer instead of dancing. There were only a few couples on the dance floor – a square of asphalt between the trees – but the band played all the louder. It was cool under the trees.

Amalia refused beer and asked for coffee. She was furious because she had on the old shoes she wore to work, and when there are only a few couples dancing, people notice a girl's legs. She saw one girl in a white dress without stockings, as if it were summer already. She could see one couple at a table in the shadows. The man had a moustache and looked a sporting type. Perhaps he was the owner of the car outside. The girl was clinging to his arm and talking to him; a typist, probably, judging from her painted finger-nails.

Tonino asked her, in his sarcastic voice, if she would like to dance.

'Not now. I'm tired,' she replied.

Tosca and Gianni were already on the dance floor. The other fellows – mechanics and apprentices, apparently – had stopped talking and were sniggering between themselves. Obviously she and Tosca had interrupted their conversation. Amalia looked at them, her face expressionless. Tonino said: 'You needn't stop what you were saying. The young lady isn't from Turin.'

A cross-eyed idiot whom Amalia did not know asked: 'Really? Where from, then?'

Another fellow remarked, shaking his head: 'A woman's a woman, wherever she comes from.' But that cross-eyed fool kept on at her until Tonino said solemnly, in an affected voice: 'We're agricultural workers, we are. Fed up with planting cabbages, so we've emigrated. Now where would our little village be, I wonder?'

Amalia pretended not to hear, but she knew he was getting at her and she felt herself sweating. For a moment her heart was louder than the band. Tonino went on: 'We're a proud lot, in our village. Won't have anything to do with people who don't work in the fields with us . . . .'

A tall curly-haired fellow came towards them, his jacket over his arm. One of the group waved and called to him. He wore a white pullover and his sunburned arms were bare. The cross-eyed chap smiled, addressing him as Remo.

Amalia sat there, looking down, while they exchanged greetings and a joke or two. Then she heard this Remo say to the others: 'Is she free?'

The orchestra started up again and Amalia jumped to her feet, throwing him a smile. They strode towards the asphalt dance floor.

Before putting his arm around her he squeezed her hand, then gripped her closely by the waist, his right hand exploring the firmness of her spine. Amalia relaxed against him, and was surprised when a little later he asked her in a low voice where she came from. She gave him an astonished smile and they said no more. When the dance was over they looked at each other for a moment. Then she said: ' You'd better put your jacket on again. It's cold.'

They walked past the couples who were still standing there, made their way to the gate and went out into the shadows of the avenue. Her companion had flung his jacket over his shoulders, his long, unhurried strides keeping him abreast of her. He did not speak, leaving the problem of conversation to her. For a moment or two, Amalia forgot he was with her, then she took herself in hand and remarked: ' I've had enough of those four ignorant fools.'

The other looked at her, then murmured: ' They're fools, all right. Don't understand a thing. What's your name?' and he took her arm.

Once again Amalia felt the same amorous squeeze as before, and gently moved his hand away. ' Let's just go on walking,' she said softly, but by the time they had reached the metalled road between the houses and the dark fields, Amalia was clinging to his elbow, listening to him telling her about last year's great race, when he and the other leading cyclists had passed the boundary line at that very spot. Amalia vaguely remembered a Sunday of shouting and uproar, and a whole flood of cyclists hunched over their handle-bars, all quite unrecognisable. Amalia had never heard the winner's name, but her companion was certainly a good dancer. She liked the way he had not boasted, saying he was riding as one of a team. ' And what are you doing now?' she asked.

He was training for a race on the Riviera. Amalia's heart

67

began to beat faster, for this meant he was an important contestant. 'The Riviera? Really?' she said.

Remo never smiled. Even in the darkness Amalia had noticed that he did not smile, not even when he stroked her thigh and told her she was a pretty girl. 'All over the Riviera?' she enquired.

Remo told her that races were won in training, and that roads were all the same. Amalia felt a longing to see him with his thighs bare. They must be very strong and well developed. She asked if he had any photographs.

Still grasping her arm, Remo suggested: 'Shall we go into the field?' They sat down in the grass, and Amalia asked when he would be going to the Riviera? Had he been there before? Remo murmured something as he ran his hand up her leg, slipped the other arm round her neck and held her close against him, kissing her. Amalia started to her feet. Remo, still squatting on the grass, looked up at her. 'But . . .' Amalia stammered, 'we hardly know each other.'

Remo stretched out his arm to seize her by the ankle, but Amalia jumped back, clearing the ditch by the bank. Far away, under the street lamp, she saw a man cycling past. Remo, still sitting in the field, cried: 'Come here, you fool! It's night-time, isn't it?'

'No! No!' Amalia cried, her heart in her mouth. 'We're not dogs.'

Cursing, Remo jumped up. Amalia ran lightly and managed to reach the street lamp. Remo followed her with great strides, but Amalia had slowed to a walk and turned aside along the pavement.

Amalia slept on a sofa in the kitchen. Her mirror and little boxes were on the chest-of-drawers in the other room where her father and mother slept. She went home only to eat and sleep. Now that the corn in front of the door was growing taller, she didn't stay at home even on Sunday mornings. The walls of the two-roomed hovel were peeling, but solidly built. The place looked like an old tavern. Amalia heartily wished the factory owners would take over the hut and the bit of land and level the lot. But her father seemed to feel secure enough, since he had sown the field.

At night, any noise outside could be heard through the door; the voices of occasional passers-by, a dog barking in the distance, the trains. With the dawn came the creaking of carts. Sometimes, but not often, the hum and swirl of a car.

This was the hut that Tosca considered more convenient than her third-floor apartment. Tosca wasn't one to go and sit in a field with a cyclist. She wouldn't even have gone there with Gianni. She was born in the town. But she would have made love in a cinema, or on a Sunday out in the country.

Amalia had done it herself in the vineyard when she was a child, but wouldn't sink to that any longer. What was the point of getting a job in the town and living her own life, if she was going to have a roll in the fields like some country wench? Anyway, love-making wasn't all that much fun, and to do it like that was disgusting. Knowing when to give way was what made her different from girls like Tosca, who would lie with any workman for the sake of a ticket to a show or a day out.

' All men are equal,' Amalia thought to herself, ' but one man isn't the same as another. That cyclist was rather nice, even if he did go off swearing in the end.' She'd have liked to ask Tosca about him. Tosca could have asked Tonino, who would have asked the others. But she was afraid they'd gossip and laugh at her. One evening she was just about to go into the *Giardino* when she saw a crowd of young fellows inside with Tonino in the middle of them, so she stayed outside, craning her neck, looking among the trees in the hope of seeing the curly-headed cyclist. There he was, wearing a polo-necked sweater, arguing with somebody and red in the face.

The very next day – it was a cold, cloudy morning – Amalia was washing herself in the dark corner of the kitchen when she glanced through the window and saw a tall man with bare legs, wearing a sweater and a white beret, leaning on a bicycle, his chin raised as he surveyed the place. It was Remo.

When Amalia went out, she kept her head down, adjusting her hat. Four steps took her along the path through the corn and into the road. She walked on without looking round, and suddenly Remo was there beside her, his bicycle clicking as he wheeled it along with one hand. He had the tanned thighs of an athlete, softened by a light covering of fair hair. Amalia was silently cursing herself for having let him pick her up at home.

'Going to work?' Remo asked quietly as they walked along.

Amalia eyed him crossly, not knowing what to say. Suddenly she snapped: 'Are you doing your training?' Then she stopped walking. At a corner in the distance, a crowd of girls and workmen waited in front of the entrance to a factory. On the chill air rose the blast of the works siren, long, discordant, imperious. 'Who told you where I live?' she asked.

'No one. I go along that way every morning,' he said, ' with my little bike. You're working today?'

'I'm in a hurry.'

'I'll call for you tonight.'

' Tonight I'm going to the theatre.'

Remo did not seem surprised. ' By yourself?' he asked.
' Then I'll come, too.'

' Don't call for me,' Amalia said. ' I'll be outside the
Giardino.'

That evening they went to the cinema instead – the one at
the town centre, because Amalia told him she was sick of
seeing the same old faces round her. Remo put on his jacket
before they climbed on the tram. They stayed quiet in the
cinema, because she stopped him and said teasingly that
there was a time for everything. The film, viewed from a
comfortable red arm-chair, interested her so much that if he
had started anything she would have been really annoyed

On their way back they stopped at a café, and Amalia
got him to talk about the race on the Riviera. He told her
about the sea, the bathers, the palm-trees. She asked if he
had ever been abroad before, wanted to hear all about his
past and his plans if he won the race.

Remo talked readily enough about his bicycle and his
races, but had very little to say about anything else. Every
now and then he tried to let his hand stray and Amalia had
to slap his fingers, blushing at the vivacity of the gesture.

She would not allow him to escort her as far as the corn-
field. She shook hands when she left him and Remo stayed
in the middle of the road, tall and a trifle round-shouldered,
watching her go into the distance.

Now the dog-days had come with their scorching heat,
and the old man was fussing round the field all the time.
When Amalia came home from work she nearly always
found him there in front of the house, testing the weight of
the ears with his hand, grubbing up weeds, then straighten-
ing up, his face radiant in the shade of his tattered old straw

hat, looking as if he had changed into one of his own corn-stalks. He would stop passers-by for a chat. Luckily, his traditional reserve kept him from telling the whole town his piffling little hopes and plans.

But he discussed them eagerly with her mother, making all sorts of calculations. He already saw himself as the owner of that couple of handfuls of land. Amalia would have given up her bottle of Cologne, if only the men who owned the factory next door would have turned them out of the cottage. Instead, her father kept on working harder than ever, going round the place several times at night and sometimes staying out until morning, so that the owners should see him there with his little lamp on his belt when they came to pick up the keys.

How was it possible that his earthy, sour-smelling body, raised between the furrow and the cowshed, could be the same flesh as her own? Amalia shuddered, thinking how he and her mother had come together – her down-at-heel mother, he with his bearded, cigarette-stained mouth on her mother's bloodless body – to bring her into the world. When Amalia washed herself, shut up in the kitchen, standing in the wash-tub, she felt she was scouring off the taint of the land and the vineyard.

Looking through the window one morning she saw her father and Remo talking together, Remo standing by his bicycle. She quarrelled violently with Remo about it and that night she did not go to meet him as arranged. Instead, the moment she had finished her supper, she ran over to Tosca's place, so that he wouldn't catch her at home if he came to the hut.

She found Tosca eating salad. Tonino was shaving. She sat down at the table facing Tosca. Tonino said he could see her in the mirror.

'You're lucky, you two,' Amalia said, 'to be by yourselves like this. All you earn is your own, and if you don't like the place you can move.'

'Why don't you make a third?' Tonino asked. 'I'd stay here.'

Tosca went on eating, looking keenly at Amalia. 'Oh, you!' she said to Tonino. 'Everybody gets fed up with their life,' she went on. 'I wish I'd been born in the country like you, Amalia. At least you're not shut in all day and if you're tired you can always lie down in the shade.'

Tonino started singing: 'Back to your village . . . .'

Amalia smiled as she looked at the salad. 'It's not all that easy: there's more work to do than there is here and nobody gives you a word of thanks. The pigs have a fine time, but not the one who looks after them. It's worse than being a servant.'

'At least you get cyclists there,' Tonino cried, half turning round, his mouth twisted under his up-turned hand.

Remo made it up with Amalia, letting her see he understood that she didn't want him coming to the house. Instead, he waited for her outside the *Giardino*. Amalia smiled as she saw him coming towards her to seize her eagerly by the wrist. Still, it hurt her a little to meet his penitent eyes as he looked down at her. Joking with Tosca at the factory, one day, she told her: 'If only he'd say a word or two!'

Remo quickly understood, too, that when they were together she didn't want to see around them faces from her own neighbourhood, so one Sunday he took her to a fashionable swimming pool where there was a string of cars outside.

They sat on the cool mosaic with their feet in the green-tinted water and smoked a cigarette. Amalia watched the bathers, envying the slim lines of their flanks, their supple spines. In her own tight costume she thought she looked plump but well built. She knew that sunbathing enhanced the attractive contrast between her skin and her hair, and a headscarf could do a lot for her. She noticed that few of the men were as well developed as Remo, and for the first time she felt a thrill in her blood as she looked at him.

Lying at full length on the sand with her eyes half shut, she thought the sun seemed more glorious, more marvellous, than on other days. Could this be the same sun that used to scorch her calves and the back of her neck as a child in the fields? Remo, stretched beside her, asked in a whisper if they could have supper together that evening. Amalia nodded without speaking.

They ended up in a room where they were served by waiters in white jackets. Amalia felt stiff after her day in the open air, and jokingly asked Remo if his training would have suffered. For the first time he laughed, revealing his teeth. ' Training gives one more strength, not less,' he told her. That day he was wearing a sports shirt and a fancy handkerchief.

' I'm a poor country girl,' Amalia babbled as she drank her iced white wine. ' You've seen where I live, haven't you? My father planted corn all round the house, as if it were a shed. If you really love me you ought to set fire to the place. At the very least, burn the corn, root it out, so that I never set eyes on it again . . . .'

She was laughing as Remo carried her bodily up the stairs of his home to an attic under the roof. He had the key of it, and kept her there till three in the morning.

In the days that followed, Amalia grew to hate that attic, the canvas camp-bed and the slanting beam that hit her head unless she was very careful. In spite of their new intimacy, Remo was no more talkative than before.

He answered crossly when Amalia remarked how nice it would be to go to the Riviera together and have a fine room and stroll on the beach. It worried her to think he was exhausting his body too much just before the race, but she knew she must bind him to her, increase his passion for her, and anyway it wouldn't have done any good to refuse him now. Instead, she must make him so used to having her that he couldn't do without her. The more so because now she, too, spent the nights in a sweat of desire. She found peace only in those thrilling moments when Remo was taking her to the attic.

One Sunday she went to Fontana Fredda on the back of a motorbike, clinging tightly to his back. There was a meeting of competitors from the whole area. Once she grew accustomed to the trick of balancing, Amalia glanced sideways at the fields flying past them. Looking at them like that made her feel happy. On their way back at sunset, facing the golden brilliance, she pressed her cheek against Remo's solid, leather-covered back, almost closing her eyes to shut out the dazzle from the roadside trees.

At Fontana Fredda, Remo talked with a man in a white suit who spoke to him like an old friend and slapped him on the shoulder. He was a Federation Technician. The following morning, Remo intensified his training and decided with Amalia that they would stop indulging in irregularities. In the evening they met for a beer or went to the cinema. Again Amalia asked if she couldn't go to the Riviera with him on the Sunday of the race, but Remo said no.

Gradually she saw him less and less – just for a moment before supper – because immediately afterwards Remo went to bed, so as to be up at dawn. His mind was full of the race and he said less than ever.

Meanwhile, the grain was swelling and turning yellow. Sparse as it was, it still waved waist-high in front of the house and the old man never left it except at night. Already, many boys had had their ears boxed for throwing stones among the corn. When Amalia went out in the morning she was ashamed to be seen.

One night when she was coming out of the cinema, all alone, she had a sudden longing to go along the road where they used to meet, so she made her way to the *Giardino*. She heard the orchestra when she was still some distance away; only as she drew nearer could she enjoy the cool shade of those trees. She halted behind the fence and looked at the crowded dance floor and the little tables; she saw the workmen sitting there. One was just coming back with Tosca, after a dance. She saw Tonino, laughing, and she saw Remo. Remo who had gone to bed three hours ago.

She felt her heart contract, and she fought down the urge to go in. After all, he wasn't even dancing. Why had he lied? He had no need to, he spoke so little. Perhaps he had felt thirsty and come down for a chat with his friends. But once the day of the race was over, she would never leave him. He meant too much to her.

If she hadn't dreaded being seen by Tonino and the others, she might still have gone in, but instead she walked on in a fury and reached home without even glancing at the rustling corn. If only that day of the race would come quickly and be over!

In the dead of night she was awakened by footsteps outside the door and the sound of heavy breathing. A dog, perhaps? Or a drunk? Terror and uncertainty kept her trembling on the sofa, her eyes starting open as she heard a coming and going, a creaking. Could it be the wind? Her heart felt numb with horror and shame at having to sleep in a low kitchen like a peasant girl, behind a door by the road, at the mercy of every passer-by; at having to keep the window bolted, even in June, for fear someone might climb in; at being alone, and knowing that Remo, too, had played her false. She was terrified in case the door was not properly shut; even worse was her dread of anyone seeing the sink in the corner with its constant dripping. She screwed up her eyes and tried to sleep.

It had not been a windy night, that much was certain. The sun was not yet up, but already the heat was oppressive. Amalia, drying herself in front of the window, saw the strip of corn all battered down and ruined. She could see the seat by the roadside, now; only yesterday it had been hidden by the yellow-green stalks.

Amalia was at the door when she heard her mother's scream at the window. They both jumped among the furrows – Amalia already had her hat on – and saw how the stalks were broken, crushed and strewn over the bare earth. A few ears were shedding their grains. A workman cycling past turned to look.

The old woman, still barefoot, was clutching her cheek with her hand, holding her elbow. ' This time your father'll murder us,' she said hoarsely.

Amalia shrugged her shoulders. She bent down and ran her hand once again through the stalks lying on the whitish soil. ' What d'you expect him to say? It must have been a drunk. Doesn't he ever get drunk himself?'

She went off, feeling sorry to leave her mother groaning there alone. She walked quickly, because groups of workmen were now hurrying past on their bicycles. Suddenly she remembered what she had said to Remo when she was drunk.

She went home again at mid-day, not letting Tosca come

with her. From a distance the hovel looked the same. Her heart began beating painfully when she saw the devastated strip. The door looked almost naked. ' Where's papa?' she cried.

The old woman was blowing the fire and looking inside the oven. ' He's gone to give notice to the factory owners. He says they did it themselves, so as to take the land away from him. He wants to go back to the village and die of hunger. Are you sure you didn't hear anything last night?'

' All this fuss for a couple of sheaves of corn, if that much. The seed cost more.'

' Go and tell that to him. You've been to work this morning?'

' He's coming back?'

' He's been back twice already. He doesn't know where to go, any more. How could you possibly not have heard something?'

When her father came back, Amalia dodged the blows, keeping her hat on and putting her gloves on the table. The old man's face was scarlet when he came in, but little by little it grew pale, limp and frightened. He went outside to rake around and came back with great tears welling from his eyes. He spilled his soup on the table. The old woman said nothing.

' Going to the factory today?' he asked suddenly. Amalia lowered her eyes to her plate. ' Work!' he went on. ' Work for those beasts! Run and join the queue! Work to fatten them! They need people like you! They make you work all day and they pay you at night. Old woman, where have you put the hoe?'

Amalia got away half-way through the meal, to stop herself from screaming. She wandered round the deserted streets in the hot sun, biting her lips and looking up whenever a tram went by the end of the road. Suddenly a cyclist shot past her, bare-legged and covered with dust. It was not Remo.

At the factory entrance, Amalia asked Tosca if she could spend the evening with her. They went shopping to buy a loaf, then they climbed the filthy stairs together and sat down in the kitchen to recover their breath. Tosca started on her housework. Tonino came home and greeted her with a meaningful nod. Amalia gave him an absent-minded smile.

While Tosca prepared the salad on the balcony, Amalia got up and began undoing a box of eggs. Tonino, who was washing himself behind a partition, said lightly: ' Aren't you even going to thank me?' His eyes and untidy hair appeared above the wooden rail. ' Don't you know I've done you a favour?'

Amalia raised her eyes. ' And if you want any grape-picking done this year, I'll be there,' Tonino concluded, coming into the kitchen rubbing his shoulder. He looked at her with a smile and his eyes grew sharp. ' They told me you wanted to see that corn cut before you could go cycling. Aren't you going to thank me?'

Amalia, leaning on the table, couldn't take it in all at once. Then her cheeks flamed and her breath died in her throat. She leapt to the door, opened it and rushed down-stairs. As she walked she hid her face, twisted with weeping, so as not to be recognised, and the shrill cries of the children reached her as from a remote distance, dulled to a faint buzzing. When she reached home she let the old man go on nagging her for a little while. Even after it was dark, he was still persisting that he couldn't make out why she hadn't heard anything from the kitchen.

(26th July – 2nd August, 1938)

The Idol

It all started again one afternoon in August. Now, whatever the sky may be, I only have to lift my head and look up between the houses to feel once more the quiet stillness of that day.

I was sitting in the little parlour that I have never seen since, where, it seems to me, only a yellowish half-light filtered through. I had come at that dead time of day to be the only one there. I still recall that when she came in I did not recognise her. All I thought was that this woman was much too thin, but I must have jumped to my feet at once, because she came across to me without the slightest hesitation and held out her hand, saying: 'How awful! It's lucky I'm dressed.' With her other hand she was buttoning her collar.

She was wearing white. A few minutes later, when she bowed her head and I felt her tears falling on my fingers, I saw where the sun had tanned the back of her neck. By contrast, her hair seemed almost blonde. I remember I managed to say: 'Let's get this straight first of all, Mina. I should be as ashamed as you of being here.'

Mina looked at me. 'It's not for shame that I'm crying,' she stammered through tense lips. 'It's just that I'm upset.'

She gave me a slow smile, but I let it die away without responding. The wrinkles at the corner of her mouth were deeper than they used to be; her old expression was now etched on her face in hard lines.

'Why d'you look at me like that?' she cried, drawing away from me. 'Trying to make me feel ashamed?'

Just then the Madame poked her head through the curtains, looked at me sharply and quickly withdrew. My eyes dropped to Mina's little slippers and the moment we were alone again I groaned, surprising myself by the sound of my own voice, 'Can this be possible, Mina? Is it possible?'

Mina gave me a quizzical look between her reddened eyelids. I looked back at her anxiously. 'Don't you fancy a sunburned girl, then?' she asked, adding as she turned away : 'I'll call another one for you.'

I clutched her shoulder. 'Let me go,' she cried shrilly, breaking away. 'Leave me alone. I'm not the sort of girl you think I am!' She rushed off through the curtains and left me standing there in the middle of the parlour.

The Madame came back and looked me up and down, severely this time. I picked up my hat and went towards the door. 'I'll come back some other time,' I murmured as I went out.

My memory of a serene deep blue sky seems to stem from that afternoon and many others that followed. When I think of it I cannot understand how the ceaseless misery that hounded me can have become linked in my mind with such lovely weather.

One Saturday, towards dusk, I was amazed to find myself strolling along those quiet streets again, well aware that my mouth was twisted in an ugly sneer. Firmly I went in and made my way to the main reception room. Mina was not there, which was almost a relief. The Madame barely glanced at me, but I was stared at by two girls sitting on the divan with their bare legs wide apart, and one of them winked at me. There were several men sitting round the walls, gazing absentmindedly at the empty floor. At the back of the room a fat, half-naked girl stood chatting with a sergeant.

Mina did not appear. 'She's working upstairs,' I thought, and found I was talking to myself, biting my lips at the excruciating pain round my heart. I went straight over to the Madame and asked for Mina.

'Who is Mina?'

I reminded her of that afternoon, and her hard lips smiled uncertainly.

'You mean Manuela, I expect. She isn't down yet. Adelaide, go and tell Manuela.'

One of the two girls led me upstairs, humming to herself and turning round to smile at me. Her long legs took the stairs three at a time, but she went slowly, waiting for me. Upstairs, doors slammed. She seemed an awfully nice girl. I thought about going with her.

'You men! You always want the girl who isn't about!' Adelaide said to me in the corridor. We went into a room that was dark and smelt like a bathroom. 'Put on the light, Manuela.'

I saw Mina stretched out on the bed, her arm raised to the light-switch and her hair over her eyes. She had on the dress she was wearing before, but her feet were bare. 'Wait a minute,' she said with a twisted grin, swinging up to sit on the edge of the bed. She thrust her feet into her slippers, ran across the room, looked around, then came back to the bed. 'You are naughty, Adelaide,' she said, turning her back as she swung on to it again. 'Naughty! Go away! Be off!'

When we were alone I looked at her in bewilderment. Under her outstretched legs was that horrible piece of coarse towelling. Near the bed, above her head, hung some light underwear. On the floor, a threadbare bedside mat.

'This is impossible, Mina. It's just impossible!'

'I was waiting for you, Guido. I knew you'd come.'

'You stayed upstairs because you were expecting me?'

Mina shook her head, smiling at me. 'No. Actually, I'm not well. These days I'm always ill. But I knew you'd come back.'

'Mina, you must tell me everything. Why are you here? Why? I can't believe it.'

Her eyes grew hard. 'There's nothing to tell you, is there? I am here, and that's enough, I should think. What d'you want to know? I was all on my own, and I looked for a job. If you want to talk to me, leave that out of it.'

'But your father, Mina. Your father? He was always telling me I was an idle slacker. Remember?' I couldn't manage to smile. 'Does your father know? I thought you were still down there ...'

'Papa's dead,' said Mina, and her eyes did not drop.

'Oh!' I murmured. 'But why didn't you write to me? Look me up? I thought of you so often. Felt sure you were married. Yet sometimes, in the morning – do you remember? – I wondered to myself, "Perhaps Mina's waiting for me".'

' "Mina's waiting for me! Mina's married!" ' she mocked. 'But you never managed to write to me. And now you're grumbling?' I lowered my eyes as her voice went on, more kindly now : 'Did you really think about me sometimes?'

'Oh, Mina!'

Somewhere in the corridor a little bell rang. 'Does the Madame know you're here?' she asked me abruptly as she started up.

'She called you Manuela when she spoke to me ...'

'Guido, you can't stay here. The Madame thinks you're a client. This is her business, you know. We'll meet again tomorrow.'

'And why can't I stay? I am a client. I'll pay as if

Manuela was some other girl. What does it cost for half an hour?'

Mina hid her face in the pillow. Biting my lips, I took out the fifty *lire* I had with me and I put them down on the chest-of-drawers. Mina's eyes followed me furtively, intently. Then she stretched out her arm and pressed the bell push three times . . .

'You're working? Earning a salary?' she asked.

I sat down on the bed. It was dreadfully hot and stuffy, and I should be sweating when I left, but at the time I did not notice it.

'I'm not well, you know,' Mina said. 'I get a pain in the kidneys if I sleep on my back. This isn't a really healthy life. Still, I went to the seaside this year and I'm better already. I ought always to live in the open air.'

The persian blinds were closed, making everything seem dark and mysterious. There was no sound from outside.

'What's the matter, Guido?' she asked anxiously, taking my hand. Without lifting her head from the pillow she gazed at me with those great eyes of hers. I squeezed her fingers to express the agony I was feeling.

'What do I matter to you?' she said calmly. 'Those things are far away, as far as Voghera. And you're married anyway, I expect.'

I shook my head. 'I shouldn't have come here.'

'But, poor boy,' Mina exclaimed, raising herself on her elbow, 'you were just looking for a woman.'

'I'm still looking for her,' I said.

Mina was not listening. 'What fools we were,' she went on. 'Still, I don't regret anything about that summer. What about you?'

'I regret the winter, when we left each other.'

Mina started laughing. I had forgotten that light laugh of hers.

'Oh, Mina!'

'Be good, now. I'm not well.'

'Just one kiss, Mina.'

'You'd be kissing Manuela.'

'Mina.'

'Tomorrow. We'll meet again then. Tomorrow morning. Perhaps I can come out. We shouldn't see each other here. Don't you feel it's all wrong, too?'

Now that it's all over, I'm sorry I was not tough enough, that day, to let her start her usual game. Even now I'm still wondering if that wasn't what she wanted. To hide the trembling of my lips I lit a cigarette.

'I smoke, too, you know,' Mina remarked, so we smoked together and went on talking. I turned my head and looked at her as she lay at full length behind me, watching me listlessly. Keeping my eyes averted from the corner of the washstand, all cluttered with towels and medicine bottles, I gradually fell silent. On the floor stood a big purple bottle.

'Give me that kiss, Guido,' Mina said abruptly. I twisted round, took her cheeks between my hands and with an effort kissed her. Her lips clung to mine and she murmured : 'It's still summer, Guido . . .' Then she broke away.

We both fell silent. I took her hand and squeezed it. Mina jumped from the bed. 'I'm too happy,' she exclaimed breathlessly. 'Too happy. Go away now. You might change. Yes, I'll wait for you tomorrow . . . And take the money you've left up there. You can probably do with it. I'm satisfied that I've seen you. I'm well paid today . . .' I looked at the money, reluctant to pick it up, and she went on : ' . . . Then give it to the Madame yourself. She should give you back twenty *lire*, so watch your change. But don't leave it here. That's right. Guido, good-bye.'

The next day I told her I wanted to marry her. Mina stopped dead, took a gasping breath of the fresh, quiet street air, and as the sounds from the pavement rose all around us she moaned, closed her eyes and murmured: 'It doesn't matter if you said it just for something to say. It doesn't matter. It's good of you.'

All that scorching Sunday afternoon I wandered round the streets, finding nowhere where I could sit and wait for the mellowing sky of evening and the return of the hour I had known the day before. Now and then I talked feverishly to myself, all alone. Towards sunset I went back to my room and threw myself down on the bed, smoking and watching the golden glow fade against the dirty windows of the house across the road.

It was dusk when I grew aware of the unusual silence and realized that for a moment I had been thinking of nothing at all. Then I felt horrified that I had asked Mina to marry me, gone out with her. Lying half-naked on the bed I let my eyes wander complacently down from my chest to my slightly sunburned legs. What was Mina's body like? I smiled cynically to think I was the only man who didn't know.

Suddenly I jumped up and dressed, my mind made up. Once again I arrived at that door, hesitant but with a forced grin, and quickly rang the bell.

This time Mina looked at me in alarm. She was standing by the door of the reception room, wearing white and chatting to the Madame. She ran over to me, shook hands and made me sit down on the sofa in the anteroom. She sat beside me, without looking at me. From the doorway the Madame gave me a faint nod.

There we sat in silence, staring down at the mosaic floor. Mina was still holding my wrist, trembling, and I was the first to look up when two young fellows went past us into the main room. 'Would you rather I went away, Mina?' I asked her quietly, finding it hard to speak.

'Why did you come?'

'I don't know.'

'Aren't you satisfied with what happened this morning?'

'I want to marry you.'

Mina smiled : 'I'm not free.'

'What?'

'I've got my work.'

I twisted round to look at her and felt my face flush.

'Hush, Guido. Go away.' There was a loud conversation in the drawing-room and a woman's shrill voice. 'Go away. We'll see each other again on Tuesday morning. Madame's watching us.'

'I've got nothing to hide.'

'Guido, I implore you. Or, rather, listen,' she went on with some reluctance, 'come back when I don't see you and ask for Adelaide.'

I grinned and shrugged my shoulders. Mina gave a sigh and watched me furtively.

'Mina,' I asked without looking at her, 'have you got a disease or something?'

'Oh, no, Guido. Why don't you understand?'

A man and a young girl came down the stairs and disappeared into the corridor. The Madame looked in.

'I just don't understand,' I said. 'Forgive me, Mina.'

'We'll meet on Tuesday. Faithfully, Guido. Now go.'

We looked at each other, and I rushed outside without a backward glance.

When I had gone a hundred yards my earlier grin was back on my lips. I walked on, muttering to myself, so tensely that my cheeks soon felt numb. The freshness of the night and the Sunday evening crowd failed to distract me. Over and over again I repeated the words I should have said to Mina, feeling more and more troubled. A great bitterness filled my mouth.

Next day at dawn, on the train taking me out of town, I found a little peace. I was dozing with the movement of the train and passively enjoying the mild warmth. With my eyes closed I could feel, under my limp, outstretched hand, the case containing my samples. This was a good trip, as all my life had been, yet there was something new about it, a pervading, indescribable and painful sweetness. At bottom, it was just as I had always dreamed it would be. From the corner of my eye I could see the fields rushing past, wakened by the first rays of the sun. I glimpsed a moment when, with my eyes still shut, I entered a new horizon where anything, no matter how dreadful or how paltry, could happen to me.

I thought about Mina waking drowsily; thought of her body still warm from my own bed, and I could not hate her. I felt grateful to her for the sweet desire that pulsed in my blood. For certain she was alone in her room; at this hour she was alone, and I could think of her. It made me smile to think of her timid suggestion that I should try Adelaide. Who knows? Adelaide and Manuela. Perhaps they were friends.

It was Tuesday morning and we met at the station. I came back on purpose to see her, though I ought to have continued my journey by car to visit certain customers up in the hills. Mina told me she was going out too often now and this was damaging her health as well as upsetting the Madame.

'Don't you need fresh air?' I murmured.

Mina made me wait for her outside a shoe-shop and came out almost at once with a small parcel. She stood on the step between the gleaming shop windows, straight and self-possessed in her little green hat and her chestnut coat with buttons at the side, her eyes glancing round in search of me. Our elbows were close together as we crossed the street.

'Where did you get your name from?' I asked.

'Don't you like it?' she replied gaily.

'Yes, it's pretty. But where did you get it?'

Mina looked up at me through her curls. 'I didn't have to look for it. It was written over the door of my room.'

We bought cigarettes that morning, then I paused in front of a stocking shop. 'If you promise me you'll wear them only on mornings like this,' I said, 'I'll buy you the nicest ones they have.'

'Come on, Guido,' she replied. 'Not here. I never buy them here.'

It was eleven o'clock and she said she must be getting back. 'Shall we sit in a café a minute, Mina?'

In the café I chose the most secluded corner and did not look up at the waiter as I gave the order.

Mina stared at me gravely, in silence, while I kept my eyes fixed on her. Then she said softly : 'You're ashamed of being out with me.'

'Mina,' I answered in surprise, 'I just want to be alone with you.'

'You don't forgive my way of life.'

'I forgive you everything that's past, Mina. Every day and every night I want to understand you. You're not the simple girl you used to be. Though I ought to grieve over so much that's happened, still, I'm not crying. I know I love you and I'm as much yours now as I was then. But marry me, Mina. Give up this life. You know you'll have to give it up some day, no matter what it costs you.'

'See? You're objecting to it. That's not forgiving.'

'D'you expect me to thank you for carrying on as you're doing now? Don't you understand what agony I endure when I'm all alone, thinking of you with all those other men?'

'But it's different with them, Guido. Quite different . . . and there aren't so many as all that.'

'I feel like murdering them !'

'Really? I know you, Guido. You'd just complain all the more if you were one of them.'

'Mina, doesn't this life make you sick?'

'I just see that you're ashamed of me, Guido. Aren't you?'

That was the first moment when I realized I was up against immense senseless power, like a man banging his head against a brick wall. Mina sat watching me, her neck bent and her eyes bright, with tiny creases between her eyebrows. I heaved a sigh and lowered my eyes.

'See what you're thinking?' Mina went on, more tenderly. 'With you, no. But it's for your own sake. I know it would be worse, afterwards.'

'Ah,' I groaned, a fearful smile trembling on my lips. 'I'll make you work myself, if you're so keen on your job. God help me, I can go with you like all the other men, can't I?'

Mina seemed taken aback. Then in a whisper, her face close to mine, she said: 'Watch yourself, Guido. If you do this, you'll never see me again afterwards.' That was the afternoon when, after wandering aimlessly for two hours in the hot sunshine through the quiet, scorching streets, I went away from Mina's door and sought out another house I knew of, at the bottom of an alley. But though I had my fill of love, the stupid, bored complacency of the girl sent me home dissatisfied, with a strong desire to weep. Besides, it brought home to me, in every detail, what Mina's work really was. Towards evening, exhausted with agony, I found myself once more outside Mina's door. I ought to have been away on my round. I remember thinking: 'If I've come back to her tonight, it means I must love her very much.'

But I didn't dare to ring. I sat down in some pub or other, almost opposite that door. Through the railing and between several pots of plants, I could see the dimly lighted entrance hall of the house, and the closed blinds masking the various rooms. 'I'll spend my evenings here,' I said to myself, but after a quarter of an hour I was as limp as a

90

rag. Every now and then some man or other, or a young fellow, a group of soldiers or a few riff-raff from the streets would disappear through that door, or, worse still, would hang around the doorstep, laughing and joking. One even arrived on a motor-bike, filling the night with hideous noise before he dismounted and ran up the steps, still in his leather jacket.

Then, the men who came out. Any one of them might have been with her. I saw a fat, bald man who looked furtively around before he vanished in the distance. If I hadn't run over then, I should have screamed.

This time I went to the door with no hesitation at all and rang at once. The room was crowded and full of smoke, but Mina was not there. I stood hardly breathing, staring at the door. Adelaide appeared, half-naked. She winked at me and gave me a military salute. I asked her if she wasn't afraid of catching a cold. Then I caught sight of Mina, taking something to the Madame. She was wearing a pale blue brassiere and white silk panties, showing her sunburned legs and midriff. Her face fell as she saw me standing behind Adelaide. She did not look surprised, merely resigned. Pushing Adelaide aside without a glance, she came over to me and was about to speak when a thin, fair-haired man with a high bald forehead, who until then had been standing idly by, walked across and took her by the hand. Lowering her eyes, Mina turned and followed him out, ignoring me completely. Adelaide giggled loudly and I felt I was choking.

Tears of bitter anguish filled my eyes, but could have passed for sweat. I heard Adelaide saying something or other, then several bells began ringing on Madame's desk and I went away, holding my head high but seeing nobody.

That evening, stupidly enough, I made another impossible resolve : to get drunk every night. I told myself : 'She's

tanned on the outside, I'll get tanned on the inside.' It
soon made me feel sick, but my nausea could not make me
forget Mina's little pale blue brassiere. Living alone, as I
did, it was hard for me to get rid of an idea, and that
sardonic, blond chap with the eyebrows was grinning at me
through the liquor fumes all night.

I saw Mina again on the following Sunday, during her
morning walk. I had waited in the pub till she left the
house, then I caught up with her in the street. She looked
surprised but stopped and shook hands with me, then said,
as if I was blocking the whole pavement : 'Let's walk on. I
don't like standing here like this.'

She complained that I had treated her badly, played her
false. She had thought a lot about me, especially in the
morning when she woke up, when she was alone. Why
wasn't I kind to her? I had been so nice at Voghera, when
I was twenty.

I did not answer, reflecting sadly that she was a woman
now. 'Played you false?' I asked abruptly. 'Who with?'

'Oh, Guido,' she replied, 'I want it, too, just as you do,
but afterwards it would be worse. You'd treat me like all
the other women . . .'

'There's one thing we can do, anyway. Let's get married.'

'Guido, I can't. This is my life, and I'm sure you'd come
to hate me in a year or even less.'

'Mina, I love you.'

'I know' she said, taking my hand. 'I know, Guido.
D'you think I don't know what you're going through? But
that's exactly why I ask you to be my friend and not want
anything more than that . . .' She looked up into my face.
'You'd be ashamed of me,' she whispered.

'At Voghera you said you'd marry me.'

'At Voghera you loved me, and believed me when I told
you Papa would not agree.'

'And you see what came of that.'

'Guido, Papa's dead, now, and the rest is my own affair.'

'You say I've been false to you. Who with?'

'Perhaps I said it because you were talking to Adelaide.'

'But she just happened to turn up. I was looking for you.'

Mina's expression clouded. 'Don't ever come to that house again,' she said. 'If you do, it's the last time you'll ever set eyes on me.'

'Mina,' I told her, steeling myself. 'I'm not going to ask anything of you, but it's obvious you feel ashamed of this sort of life, so why not give it up and let's get married? I'm the same as I always was.'

'I've got nothing to be ashamed of. I've told you that before.'

'Have you got syphilis, Mina?'

She burst out laughing. 'How could I work if I had? Oh, Guido, what a boy you are! It would be grand if we could be just good friends and forget everything else. What difference does it make to you? Just pretend I'm already married.'

We met several times after that, always in the morning. Mina would wear her green and chestnut outfit, but once she came in white, looking taller and more sophisticated in her swirling cape. To make it possible for me to spare two or three mornings a week, I began doing my travelling at night, skimping my rounds and leaving out some of my customers altogether. Some evenings as I jumped on the train by myself I longed to have Mina with me, so tall, so serene. Yet this vision could not efface my other impression of her. It was only a question of clothes. Strip her, and she would look as she always had. The very thought of how her lovely little brow wrinkled when she felt uncertain, made me tremble. Days when I knew she was going bathing were agony to me. I imagined her going there all by herself and in thought I went with her, full of tenderness; sat by her, walked beside her, whispering words of love; till we fell asleep side by side. Sometimes I got over the horror of those tedious afternoons by persuading myself that everything was all right; that I had found a new woman, unsullied in her humiliation. Her very firmness in resisting me seemed something to appreciate, a bitter-sweetness. It gave me a vague feeling of comfort to reflect that her inmost, secret life was lonely and proud. I felt she was my equal.

One chilly morning in September when she came to meet me, she brought a younger girl with her, a kid with too much lipstick and a hat pulled down over one eye. I think I must have looked disappointed, because they both looked at each other and started laughing. The girl's laugh was loud and deep.

'Aren't we still going to have a meal together?' I murmured to Mina as I fell into step beside her.

'Let's go,' she smiled, taking my arm. She skipped along, clinging close to me. I was surprised and delighted, because that day I had a lot of things I meant to tell her in our quiet hour over lunch. But the presence of the girl dried me up.

Mina started talking to me about my work and made me list the places I had been to in the last few days. She frowned when I explained, half-smiling, how I had cut out certain clients rather than miss her free mornings. She stopped dead on the pavement, and made a face at me. My smile faded and my eyes pleaded with her to get rid of her companion, stuck there with us.

'You'll ruin yourself by tricks like that,' Mina said dryly, 'and I don't want this to happen. I can't bear to hear of such stupid pranks. When anybody is working, they ought to work. You're on your own, with your own way to make. It means I'm ruining you, then, and we shan't see each other any more.'

Stupidly, a smile flickered over my lips again. I glanced at the profile of the other girl, who was passively staring at the ground. I did not answer Mina except by taking her arm and muttering 'Let's walk.' Mina broke away and we moved on.

After a long silence, the other girl abruptly asked her something. Adelaide had used two dozen tablets of violet scented soap in a month, and they discussed whether the Madame was justified in making so much fuss about it.

'What did she do with them?' I enquired.

'She didn't do anything with them, see?' the girl grinned, showing wrinkles at the corners of her mouth. 'That woman's just a silly fusspot.'

I looked at Mina who was staring down at the cobblestones. I compared her profile with the thin, sensual face of the other girl and noticed again its clean line and the firmness of her chin that I loved. I stroked her arm gently and squeezed it against me.

'Have you known each other long?' I asked the girl.

'Nuccia comes from Romagna,' Mina replied.

Ignoring me, Nuccia remarked to Mina, 'I've been working at Madame Martire's place in Bologna. She'd like to have you back there again.'

I shuddered. Mina looked Nuccia straight in the eyes. We quickened our steps and in silence reached the café where Nuccia had someone waiting for her.

At the little white table in our own eating-house, Mina and I looked at each other without speaking. I noticed that her hands had lost their sunburn.

'Were you very sunburned?'

'I got a lot of sunbathing. I used to take a boat, go out to sea and strip off my costume.'

'You go rowing on your own?'

'It isn't hard.'

I stared at her. Mina gave a tentative smile. 'Don't say anything, Guido. I go out to sea to have a rest.'

'But I was thinking of coming with you.'

'That's just it. But I go there for a rest.'

Mina's plate was soon empty. As she watched me through lowered eyes, she said suddenly: 'Why do you do those things?'

'What things?'

'Why do you shirk your work? How can I trust you if that's what you do?'

'What about you? You won't marry me?'

'I've told you already, Guido.'

'No, you haven't. You just like fooling me. When are you going to Bologna?'

'I'm not going to Bologna. Perhaps I'll go to Milan.'

'How many of these houses do you go round to?'

'I've never thought of listing them.'

'Is some man keeping you? Who?'

Mina's hard look softened. 'You must have suffered a great deal, Guido, to say things like that to me. I think they hurt you, too.'

'If I'm going to be hurt, I prefer it this way. You don't want me because you've got some other man.'

'But, Guido, don't you see how I work, the sort of life I lead? If some man was keeping me . . .' she said sadly, then suddenly frowned. 'I keep myself, and you know it.'

'It's because I see the life you lead, that I want to marry you. Oh, Mina, can't you understand me, or is it that you won't? We could work together, if you like; see each other only in the evenings; if you don't want to, we won't get married, but give up this life, have pity on me, you're the only woman worth the trouble. Even in the old days, at Voghera, you wouldn't listen to me when I begged you. Tell me how I should plead with you now. This life your are leading . . .'

'I like the life I'm leading,' Mina said calmly.

My face fell. I could have hurled a stone at her. Dazedly

I looked around me, struggling to control myself in my keen agony. Then a wild fury rose in my heart, and keeping my voice low I flung at her every insult I could think of.

'You see? And you wanted to marry me,' Mina remarked.

One morning she unexpectedly asked to see my room and put it tidy for me. Nervously I took her up the old, gloomy staircase and threw open the window as soon as we were inside. With fresh air and light there came a new awareness. On the floor lay my gaping suitcase near the half-open cupboard, and a pile of old catalogues from my firm. The dirty coffee cup on the side table and the untouched bed were just as I had seen but scarcely noticed as I went out a little while ago. Mina walked over to me and kissed me. Even today, when it's all over, I still tremble at the memory of the pure, firm sweetness of her hidden body. All the time, Mina gazed at me with her limpid eyes, caressing my spine. There was a fresh atmosphere about it all, such as I have never known since.

But the afternoon came and I was left alone. Mina had promised to say she was ill that day, provided that I went off to work. I nodded, and caught the train, but after one full day away I was back again at dawn. I wrote her a little note and handed it in to the foul-mouthed doorkeeper of the brothel, who opened the door in her dressing-gown and accepted it with a bad grace. Everyone in the house was still asleep, and I ran off to wait for her in our café. The streets were veiled in a slight fog. The trees in the avenues were still green, but cold.

I was already biting my nails when Mina arrived, some time later. She came in without looking at me, wearing green and chestnut. She sat down, then raised her eyes.

'Mina, you're here,' I said softly.

'Why have you called me, Guido?'

I stammered : 'I came back to see you, and my firm's gone bankrupt. This very day,' I moaned, clenching my fist.

'Should I believe you?'

'Why should I lie to you? It's my loss.'

'How did you hear about it?'

'I looked in this morning to report and I saw the notices. I've been aware for some time they were a bit shaky, but I didn't think . . . Perhaps they may still make some sort of settlement.'

'And you? What will you do now?'

'I'll live on my savings. I've got a little. I'll look for something else. We ought to get married and look for something together.'

'Oh, poor Guido. Now you'll have to think of work.'

'Won't you help me?' I said, feeling disappointed.

'Of course I'll help you. But you shouldn't think about me any more, not in this way. Have you anything in mind?'

I watched her drinking her coffee, looked at her eyes, seeking for the Mina of yesterday. 'All the evening I dreaded that you might go down,' I told her, stroking her hand.

'I did go down, my dear . . . to supper.'

'You see, Mina, I can't get that fellow out of my mind – you remember him – the one you went off with that Tuesday evening when you were jealous of Adelaide. A languid sort of chap, wearing glasses. I was thinking, perhaps he's back again today. Who knows?'

Mina half-closed her eyes, thinking. Then she made a face. 'I remember . . . You were a bad lad that evening. Why did you come? I was very hurt about it.'

'And what about me, Mina? But hasn't that fellow been back again?'

98

'Why him in particular?'

'Oh, Mina! With him I saw you play me false.'

'Play you false,' Mina smiled. 'Can I play any man false?'

'You can give him hell, if you want to.'

'What about yesterday, Guido? Was that hell?'

It was lovely that morning, as we sat by the window in the sunshine. Lovely, but my hands were trembling. In the end Mina noticed it and asked me: 'What's the matter with you? Why are your hands shaking?'

'They need a ring to hold them still.'

Mina laughed aloud, diverted by my little joke. 'You're a dear when you say things like that,' and she gave me a smile.

From that day on I lived like a lunatic, spreading out my journeys and trying to do a week's work in a single day, calling at offices where they rarely saw me, or shook their heads and threatened to throw me out. That month I should get barely half my usual commission. I spent long afternoons dreaming of the future, dreaming of Mina in her white dress, trying to suppress my own vivid and recent memories of her nakedness. The evening, especially, was a long drawn out agony that forced tears to my eyes, moment after moment. I could not endure it. I groaned aloud, with no one there to hear me. Sometimes I drank, but then my tears and groans broke out worse than ever. I drank till I was sick, but could not gain oblivion and at last fell into a restless doze, embracing my pillow.

My pitiless darling came back to me every now and then, treating me tenderly, obdurate only if I asked her to marry me. It made me feel so cheap that I felt reluctant to let her see the state I was in, or to ask her again. I dreaded to see the look in her eyes when I did so, or to hear her harsh reply: 'If you love me, understand me.' Sometimes the intolerable agony would wring a protest from me, whereupon she would smile sadly. I tried to treat it lightly but thought of killing her. I told her so, through my clenched teeth.

Since she now thought I was unemployed I waited for her every morning and went with her to do her shopping. I wouldn't have missed it for anything. Sometimes I tried to pay for something she had bought, but she would never let me. When I was alone I would walk to and fro in front of the shops where she had bought perfume or linen, trembling at the thought of her.

'Mina,' I murmured one day when we had been together, 'when I look at you or you look at me, your eyes are almost closed. Someone once said that when women do that they roll up their eyes so that only the whites can be seen. Don't you do that?'

'The things you think of!' she smiled with her cheek against mine.

'It's because I love you,' I replied softly.

'If you love me, that should be enough for you,' she said, holding me close.

As we went downstairs that day we found no need of words. It was raining and we walked arm in arm, close against the wall. I knew that any moment now I should be alone again, and shivered in anticipation.

'What's the matter, Guido?'

'Nothing. I'm quite happy.'

'Look here, Guido, do you remember what Nuccia said that day?'

'What? That you're going to Bologna?'

'No, Guido, to Milan,' she gave me a twisted smile. 'What she said first, when she was talking about Adelaide.'

I didn't remember.

'She said the Madame treated Adelaide badly. D'you remember now?'

I nodded, and she went on : 'Guido, we're all a bit like

Adelaide. It comes from the life we lead. It's not too good a life, Guido.'

Staring straight in front of me but seeing nothing, I broke the silence : 'With Nuccia, Mina?'

'What does it matter who with?'

I felt a strange sense of relief and humiliation. I found it hard to breathe the damp air and stood clinging to Mina's arm without realizing it. For no reason at all, we halted at the corner.

'Now are you disgusted?' Mina asked, her wide-open eyes staring into mine.

'Oh, Mina. Anything you do is all right with me. D'you know,' I went on, letting go of her arm, ' perhaps I like it this way. I prefer it.' Mina gave me a sidelong smile and went away.

Two days later we left for Milan. I had convinced her there was nothing more I could do in Turin, and I might perhaps have found a job up there with a firm of competitors. We stayed in the hotel and Mina spent two days and nights with me. Whenever I had been in Milan before I had always been passing through, and those two days were like a dream. We walked through long, unfamiliar streets, clinging to each other, looking at the shops and going back at night with shining eyes. It filled my whole heart, that temporary room all cluttered with suitcases, but quiveringly alive with Mina's constant presence. Those were the last, serene days of October, when trees and houses were still full of mild warmth.

Then Mina went away into the brothel. I wrote to ask my employers whether they would put me in charge of this new territory. They replied that unless I resumed work in my own sector they would at once relieve me of my job as their representative. I did not even reply and started looking for new employment in the city.

November came with its rain and fog. I was living at

the end of a courtyard in an airless room. There were no
women about and I never made my bed. I never cleaned
the place unless Mina was coming, but she seldom did
come because she was too tired in the mornings. I spent
hours at a time stretched out on the bed, listening to the
rain, and later on watching the snow. I still had a thousand
lire or so, but I missed my meals in the hope that the
money might be used to marry us. I was tormented by
harsh, rebellious thoughts whenever I wandered round the
streets, numb with cold, envying the street-cleaners who
at least had a job.

Mina stayed in a forbidding-looking villa at the end of a
road that opened on a dull little park. There were carpets
inside and the place was very warm, as I found one day
when I escorted her to the entrance. The price was higher
here, and a new rage began to burn in me. The visitors
were rich men with more leisure, many of them old. She
told me so herself. I'd rather have known she was in the
arms of a soldier or some factory-worker. I could have
gone there like any other man, but there was no question
of that; some nights I wept with rage, but the memory of
her hostile glance was enough to hold me back. I was
alone – I told her so, once – I never found another woman;
the city was so huge and strange it put me off; on some
grey afternoons I was so cold I could have cried; couldn't
I come and find her?

'If you had stayed in Turin . . .' she said, then added
quickly. 'If you came once you'd come another time, and
another, and you need all your savings.'

'If I came only for a chat, Mina?'

'No. I'll soon come to you.'

One evening as I was eating a plate of soup in a café,
I heard two people, a man and a woman, talking about an
agency that worked wonders. I had lost all hope of a
representative's job, but it then occurred to me that I

might find temporary work. We talked about it over a couple of glasses of wine. I watched their faces with infinite care. All through that period, except when I was tortured by jealousy, I felt a kind of humble tenderness when two human eyes gazed into mine. The girl was thin, with her hair hanging over her eyes and wearing a shabby mackintosh; the man, a gaunt workman, sucked gently at a cigarette. They had been out of work for months, but now he was doing a gardening job. This was the first meal they'd been able to buy. The girl said nothing but sat there nodding, devouring me with her eyes.

Next morning I rushed round to the agency, but they had nothing at the moment.

We went back to our own town at the end of March. My old landlady had kept my room for me, but I was almost ashamed to let her see my bony face. I had become the sort of man who trembles at an unexpected word.

Mina was talking of taking a holiday and playing around for a while. Her cheeks were a little sunken now; her lips were too pale and she used lipstick; the wrinkles on her forehead were deeper. She talked to me most tenderly and asked me if I still loved her.

But she went back to the house where she had been before, though I begged her not to. It was as much as her life was worth. She should go to the country for a short time, think of herself, for a change. I would stay in Turin to look for a job. All she would say was that for the first few days she would not come downstairs to work, and in fact she often came out with me for the evening, but one afternoon when I ventured to go in to look for her they told me she was working. Slowly I made my way back home.

I found casual work, where I had to wear overalls to save my ordinary clothes. I washed cars from dinner-time on, all through the night, in a garage not too far from where

I lived. I still remember those long hours of waiting, when I sat on the bench outside, furtively smoking under the red light of the huge neon sign. Now and then some travelling salesman whom I had once known would drive in, but I avoided them all, for fear of having to talk about myself. Often enough I was quite happy, sitting there alone.

Mina would come out in the mornings, wearing a striking, flame-coloured cloak that made her stand out from the crowd, even at a distance. Her laughter-wrinkles gave her a young, gay look, like a leaf on an orange. She soon regained her bloom and developed the tantalizing habit of closing her ears to anything I said. It made her seem even more of a darling. The only indication of her inflexible determination was in the tone she unconsciously adopted when she talked about us. She was a year older than I was, and to me she seemed grown-up, superior, more mature. Compared with her, what was I but a scatter-brained boy?

We talked about that August day when I first asked her to marry me. 'I loved you for that, too,' she told me. 'The day comes when one wants a home of one's own. You gave me a feeling that I should have laughed at, once. I wish I could go back to what I was at Voghera, young and silly, but worthy of you. If only we hadn't parted then, Guido!'

'But we've found each other again, Mina. We're sure of one another. When I think of this I don't regret your past.'

'You'd regret it one day.'

'Mina, have I ever once reproached you about your past? It's the present that's killing me. Oh, Mina, now we know we could stay together. Those two days in Milan . . .'

'But you've got to work, now. You can't be thinking about women . . .'

Another time, when I was on my way back to my job and gritting my teeth to endure another night of jealousy,

Mina said to me : 'You forget I've got all sorts of vices.'

'We'll take care of any vices,' I replied with a shrug, but we were both embarrassed as we exchanged a glance.

April, that year, brought none of its usual sweetness. The weather was chilly, almost cold. Rainclouds hung, every morning, above the tender green trees in the avenues. It rained often, the fresh, warm, whispering rain of spring. In my bare little room, I sometimes gazed at Mina in agony. She would give a start of surprise, compose herself and make some remark or other. Once I asked her what vices she had meant. 'Silly boy,' she cried, holding out her hand to me. 'Why must you always take me seriously?'

At last the sun broke through and a light wind freshened the streets. I thought I should soon be able to take Mina to the seaside for a rest. I had never seen the sea in spring-time.

One morning I was in the pub opposite the house, not expecting to see her, just watching the sunshine slanting against the cobblestones and thinking of her asleep behind those closed blinds. All at once three figures came through the front door; a man and two women. The second woman, in blue and orange, was Mina. They passed along the pavement in front of the tubs of flowers. The other woman was Adelaide. I hardly recognized her in her little hat. The man had a jutting profile and was wearing glasses. His hat was pulled down on his forehead. He was walking arm in arm with Mina and I saw his face – the face I had hated ever since that August evening.

Next day I asked Mina about him, hardly managing to bring out the words. Mina told me it was indeed the same man. Quite casually she explained that he had come back again one evening and had taken a fancy to Adelaide. The two were now good friends. Then another girl named Mafalda, had taken him upstairs with her, leaving the other two girls alone. Adelaide had told Mina a lot of silly, sentimental nonsense about the poor fellow, an engineer. Mina started explaining to me how shy he was, but I harshly interrupted her: 'Did you ever go upstairs with him?' I asked in a choking voice.

Mina shrugged. 'He's a good client.' After a moment she went on: 'He wants to marry me.' She looked straight at me, then dropped her eyes. 'Now, Guido,' she murmured, her voice hard. 'Don't be a silly boy.'

I thought I had learned a bit about suffering, but that day it was like a hurricane. I knew why a man winds his cape round his throat so as not to suffocate. It's like being in a raging wind that catches your breath. Alone in my room, leaning against the wall, my every breath was a groan. I was amazed that I did not cry aloud, that I did not fall as if struck by a thunderbolt, my eyes starting from my head. I could not call out; I could not move; I just stood there choking for perhaps half an hour. Something within me was burning to ashes.

When I went out, towards evening, I was feverish and dazed. I was well aware that nothing had really changed; that the streets lay peaceful in the setting sun, people were walking up and down, night was falling and tomorrow I should see Mina as usual; I knew I was alive and unharmed, yet I looked around me frantically as if I had gone mad and the whole world had turned topsy-turvy.

Next day I asked her another silly question. 'Why did you say yes to him?'

'But I haven't said yes to him,' Mina replied.

'But you took him inside with you, which means you accept him.'

'Who knows why?' she laughed.

'Does he know you're called Mina?'

She dropped her head remorsefully. 'You see? I'm no good.'

By now my savings had dwindled and at the garage

I earned barely enough to keep me. I reflected that now, even if she were willing, I couldn't have married Mina. I was seized with a blind rage against that blond lout. Either he had plenty of money or, since he went there to find her, she was keeping him herself. I said so to her once, and she answered : 'He's a decent man, just unlucky. He's a real friend to me and doesn't make scenes as you do. You're only a boy, Guido. Why don't you go back to your job?'

'But I haven't got it any more, you know that.'

'I was so proud of you, when you travelled around.'

'You mean to kill me, Mina?'

She came to see me again, one morning in May. We stayed together a long time and I watched her trembling. She clung to me like a mother, then pushed me away. 'Happy, Guido?' I told her I was, and she went on : 'You see, my dear, you should always remember me as I was that day. You've always said you forgave me. If I've made you suffer, think that I've suffered too, because of you. Perhaps more than you. Because I love you very much.'

'Mina, shan't we see each other any more?'

'Of course we'll see each other, but not here. I do you harm by coming here. You should be thinking of your work.'

'But without you, Mina . . .'

'With me, Guido. We'll see one another every morning . . .'

'And if you marry him?'

'I haven't decided yet.'

'Let me come to you, too. Then we shall fight on an equal footing.'

'But he hardly ever comes.'

There were certain empty mornings when Mina did not keep her appointment, which meant that someone had gone to find her when she was still in bed. I would sit there

endlessly in the café, saying nothing, staring at the empty
air, hardly hearing the traffic. The whim took me to affect
a smile; even when I could no longer keep it up, the lines
of it were fixed on my lips. I felt as if I were always
drunk.

One evening I felt I could no longer breathe. All the
afternoon I had wandered round, my eyes full of tears.
I should have gone down to the garage, but instead I went
to find Mina. I rushed up those three steps, trembled as
I rang the bell and went into the room with that smile on
my face. I shouted: 'Scum! The whole lot of you!'

They seemed to take it as some new form of greeting
and nobody moved. The girls, Mina among them, were
sitting near the door talking among themselves and they
barely turned round. Instead, one of the men sitting beside
them looked up sharply and stared at me. I glanced along
the row of them, looking for that face. I could have
murdered him.

But that face was not there. Mina followed me with her
eyes, came up behind me and said softly: 'D'you want to
go up with me, Guido?'

I followed her like a man in a dream. Going up the stairs
I thought about the day I went up them behind Adelaide,
before any of this had happened. Mina went into the same
room as before. 'Manuela' was written on the door.

On the chest-of-drawers were two large suitcases, open
and empty. The bed was neatly made. The room was full
of a light perfume, with an underlying hint of soap and
rubber. As she closed the door she asked, without turning
round: 'Who were you looking for, down there?'

I replied quietly: 'I wanted to kill that fellow. You know
the one. And if he does come I will kill him, even though
it'll do me no good now. Oh, Mina . . .' and I fell to the
floor in front of her, clasping her knees.

'You see?' she said nervously, not bending down towards

me, 'You see? It's no use. Don't make me cry. You can see I'm going away.'

'You're going to Bologna?'

'No. This time it's for always. Get up. I'm going to be married.'

She said it calmly and simply, her voice quite under control, and I realized the utter futility of my position. I rose to my feet and looked around the room in complete bewilderment, gazing at the mirror, the cluttered seat, a crack in the door. 'I shall suffer later,' I told myself. 'Later, when I'm alone.'

'Do you want me?' Mina asked, bending her head to look intently at me and sliding her silk dress off her shoulders.

I'm sorry, now, that I didn't take her, tear her to pieces, destroy her. Perhaps if I had I could have got her out of my mind afterwards. Instead, the pain of that moment comes over me again even today, and I feel like a whipped dog.

Mina stood looking at me and stroking her shoulder. I stared back at her and said bluntly : 'Don't undress yourself, Mina, if you mean to get married.'

Glowing with happiness she came over to me and took my hands, holding them close to her heart. 'Forgive me, Guido. Now I know you really and truly love me.'

'I made another sacrifice for you, once.' Her eyes flashed, and I went on : 'Remember I told you my employers went bankrupt? Well, they didn't. I just wanted to be free to follow you.'

She let my hands fall. 'You did that?'

'Yes.'

'Stupid! Why don't you go back? Oh, you're such a fool! Why did you do it? Why did you want to ruin yourself? What a boy you are! Go back! Just a boy. A silly boy.'

When I left her, those words reverberated endlessly in my brain. All night they never stopped.

The suffering that followed was beyond description. But the next morning I no longer expected Mina in the café. I no longer called at the house to see her. There was only one thing I would have liked to tell her, that left me blazing. Even now it chokes me when I think of the past. 'He got rid of your vices for you, I suppose?'

For a long time I felt shattered, as when I used to cry myself to sleep when I was a child. I thought of Mina and her husband as two grown-ups with a secret. A boy can only watch them from a distance, unaware of the joys and sorrows that make up their life. I found work in my garage for the long mornings, too, and little by little I learned to resign myself, as the summer went by. Now that I've grown old and have learned how to suffer, Mina has gone.

The Leather Jacket

My father lets me spend my days hanging round the café at
the boat-hire station because he thinks that way I can amuse
myself and unconsciously learn a trade at the same time.
A fat woman owns the place now, and she's always grous-
ing. If I as much as touch a boat she sees me every time,
even when she's down in the storeroom, and shouts at me
to leave other people's property alone. Behind the café are
some little tables and chairs for the customers, but this new
owner doesn't employ an assistant. If I take in an order
she sends her son out with the glasses. There's a part of the
café I'm not allowed into any more, nor can I go upstairs
to look at the water and the boats from the window of
Ceresa's room. Hardly anyone comes to the place now, and
my father must be crazy if he still thinks I can learn a job
here.

This Madame Pina had no idea how to manage things.
The customers treat her just as they do me. There's a lot
more to running a business like that than just putting on
a leather jacket. You've got to make people like coming.
If you're the owner you must look proud of your boats and
the River Po, show your customers you think it's a fine
thing for them to enjoy themselves that way.

That's just the sort of man Ceresa was, always joking
with everyone and more at home in the boats than his

customers were. When Ceresa was here there was always
something to laugh about; he would wade about in the
water in his bathing trunks, baling out the boats, touching
up the seams with pitch when they needed it, and in good
weather he would take the trouble to put a basket of grapes
on the tables under the trees.

The girls who went boating always used to stop by the
shed for a laugh and a chat. One of them was always
pestering Ceresa to take her up the river, but he just told
her he couldn't leave the café and the landing-stage. 'You
should come along one morning before the sun is up,' he
teased, and one morning the silly girl actually did! 'If you
get up as early as this every morning,' he told her, 'you
won't have those headaches you talk about.'

Ceresa always wore the leather jacket that now the old
woman throws over her shoulders when it rains. Once, I
remember, when we were out in a boat and a storm blew
up, he took it off and told me to wrap it round myself.
Under it he was always bare to the waist, and he used to
tell me that if I spent my life on the Po I'd have muscles
as strong as his when I was a man. He had little moustaches
and he was out in the sun so much his hair was almost white.

A year or two ago, one or two customers stopped coming,
on account of Nora. To begin with she was just a waitress
who took people their drinks, and she went away at night,
but, before long, no matter how late I went home she was
still in the café, and when I got there in the morning she
was already looking out of the window. She wasn't a
pretty girl – not that Ceresa ever said so, but that's what the
other young fellows said, and so did the old men who
came to play bowls. Nora would stand leaning against
the door, cupping her elbow in one hand, wearing a red
dress and staring at everybody without saying a word.
Once, when I was sitting on the steps waiting for Ceresa,
she said to me : 'Get along home, you fool.' But at other

times she would laugh to see me sitting in a boat with my feet in the water, and if anyone wanted an oar or a cushion when Ceresa was not about, she would tell me to go and fetch one from the shed.

It suddenly troubled me that Nora no longer left the café. At first, when I remembered her, I would say : 'She's a pretty girl,' and think no more about it. But if she was now keeping Ceresa company, it meant there was something quite extraordinary about her, and this worried me because I didn't understand what it could be.

They took their meals together under the awning, and I would stay around for a while to help them if any boats came back, so that they did not need to get up. They would talk together, giving me a word every now and then, but most of all they would gaze into each other's eyes or wink at one another. If Nora went into the kitchen to take away a plate, Ceresa would sit in silence, watching the door. They talked to each other in a way they did not talk to me. Ceresa, who joked with everyone else, never did with her; instead he would talk softly, tapping the point of his finger on the table and looking down. Or he would play with the zip fastener of his jacket as if it were a fan, and Nora would screw up both her eyes and laugh as she watched the zipper.

It was understood that they stayed together for company, not with the intention of getting married, for Nora never wore the sort of clothes housewives wear at home. She had her red dress and an even prettier white one, and once she had washed up and swept the place she would stay by the door or come over to look at the water as girls do when they come to hire a boat. When Ceresa came looking for her he would stroll lazily along as though he had nothing to do, but actually there was plenty to do and the days were long : she served in the café, washed his shirts and still found time to smoke a cigarette.

Nora was the mistress now. Ceresa told me that one day
we would take a boat, he and I, and go up the Po beyond
the weir, staying away until the evening. Nora never came
out in a boat with us. She always said the water was too
rough, and when we went off with nets and a basket to fish
under the bridge she would watch us from the window and
laugh. When he was going fishing, Ceresa never wore
anything but his jacket and a little pair of very tight bathing
trunks. We would jump in the water and fix the basket
between the stones, then I would hold the boat steady while
Ceresa stirred up the fish with his hands. He knew a
wonderful lake up beyond the weir, where he could always
fill the basket. He promised we would go up there one
fine day and not come back till evening. Many mornings
I arrived at the landing-stage hoping this would be the
right day, but it always turned out that there was a job
waiting to be done, or he had to tell Nora something, or
he had to caulk a boat where a seam had opened the night
before, so our outing was put off.

In the end I went up there by myself, to that lake
beyond the weir. One day Ceresa had something to do in
Turin so I stayed with Nora. She was washing some greens
in a bucket by the shed, watching me all the time but
saying nothing. I soon felt bored, so I told her I was taking
a boat out and off I went. I stayed on the water till midday,
thinking as I came back that I shouldn't see Ceresa that
day so I might as well go home. But I was wrong. Ceresa
was back already, slipping on his jacket by his bedroom
window. He smiled at me and called me up. I took a step
forward, but then I saw Nora blocking the door and
scowling at me, so I was afraid to push past her and go
upstairs. I told her: 'Ceresa called me up', but she didn't
move so I went into the shed to put the oars back. Nora
looked at me for some moments, then went upstairs herself.

The mornings were the best time, because then one could

always hope something nice was going to happen, more than in the evenings. Now I was sent home in the evening, because after supper Ceresa and Nora would dress up and go off arm in arm for a walk or to a cinema in Turin. They would shut up the café even before it was really dark and leave the landing-stage deserted. At first there was usually some customer or other waiting to be served, but Ceresa would send him away. He never felt the cold and generally wore shorts, even after dark. It made me furious that Nora, who never went out in the sun and must have been as pale as the belly of a fish, should treat him as an equal, and walk arm in arm with him. I would have given a good deal to know what they talked about.

'When I get married,' Ceresa said to me one morning, 'It'll be the same as before, you'll see.' I was holding the pitch for him just then and felt like bursting into tears. I didn't cry, though, but kept my eyes on the boat, for he was smiling. I was careful not to let Nora hear me from the kitchen. 'I shouldn't get married,' I said softly, though I knew perfectly well he'd made up his mind to marry her. 'If you do, Nora won't go on wearing her red dress and you'll start quarrelling.'

'What were you talking to Zucca about yesterday while he was playing bowls?'

Ceresa always knew everything that was going on. Zucca, the one with a goitre, had remarked to another man that Nora was as obstinate as a mule and Ceresa had better not marry her. All I had done was to listen as I brought them their drinks.

'You're just a boy,' Ceresa told me. 'You shouldn't bother about what grown-ups say. But if Nora tells you anything, let me know.'

But Nora never told me anything that mattered. Often enough she drove me away. When we were working on a boat, Ceresa and I, she would watch us from the door as if she were the boss, and I never knew whether she was looking that way at me or Ceresa. By now I was only waiting for him to bring the subject up again, to tell him Nora was a bad lot.

A few days after that business about Zucca I was sitting in a boat, waiting for Ceresa to come down, but he did not come. He had slipped upstairs a couple of minutes ago to fetch something to smoke, but it was a fine evening and there might well have been a customer to detain him. I was watching his open window from the water's edge but had not seen him come down. It had been a warm afternoon and so still that I could not even hear the water lapping against the boats. Suddenly I saw Ceresa standing with his back to the window, talking to someone in the room, but he did not turn round or say anything to me.

So I sat there looking at the sun, screwing up my eyes and seeing so many red and green streaks that in the end I got tired of them. I waited I don't know how long, but at last I saw Ceresa by the shed, lighting a cigarette and calling to ask me if we were doing anything. I showed him the oar, and he made a gesture as if he didn't feel like going fishing after all, but he jumped into the boat and sat there saying nothing, just letting me take him down to the bridge. Then he dropped into the water and we started fishing. Every now and then he muttered something about the fish, still smoking and staring down into the water. I spoke of a motor-boat that went by and then asked him if it ran on petrol, but he didn't go on talking as he generally did. He just tipped the little fish into the bottom of the boat and mumbled : 'You're no good, either.'

That evening, Zucca went past in his boat and called out: 'Hello, there.' I went on pouring water over the fish and said : 'You're a sly one, all right.' Ceresa looked at him, then with a smile at me, putting his hand on my head and rubbing my hair up the wrong way.

Yet he hadn't quarrelled with Nora, so far. Women like kicking up a fuss, or at least bursting into tears. They're different from us. But with Nora everything was quiet. I'll swear that sometimes Nora actually said to him, as she did to me : 'What a fool you are ! Out of my way !' but all Ceresa did was to twist her wrist and push her away. Once, in front of two customers he asked her to sew up a cushion that had got torn in a boat. Nora took the cushion and threw it in the water. Then she shut herself away upstairs and would not open the door.

I started waiting on customers at the tables behind the café, where nobody had noticed anything. Ceresa did not speak to me at all the rest of the day. He stayed in the shed, mending a rowlock, working the forge by himself, then picking up the coals with his hands and throwing them into the Po while they were still so hot that they hissed as they struck the water.

Next day I found the door shut. I called, but no one was there, so I went away because I didn't want customers to find me there and have to tell them Ceresa had quarrelled. The landing-stage was dead for two whole days. Then one morning as I was wandering along the river bank I saw movement among the boats. Ceresa was back; Nora had come back, too, and was standing by the window, changing her blouse. Ceresa was helping a couple of girls into a boat, some of those who generally undressed in the shed, shouting a lot of stupid nonsense. Ceresa was laughing and holding the boat for them.

There was a party that night because Nora had come back. Five or six customers and other boatmen came along – Zucca, Damiano, the usual crowd – but they seemed gayer than normal and stayed there talking and laughing till midnight. They all said that Nora ought to go bathing. Tomorrow they would buy her a bathing costume and she would wear it when she waited on the ones who played bowls. Then the moon came out and the bank was as bright as noonday. Damiano brought some wine and they started playing cards. I was fit to drop with tiredness, but did not want to go away, until Nora said to me, (or I think she did), 'Aren't your family expecting you home?' so I left.

From that day on, Nora seemed nicer and happier, but she was always quick to answer Ceresa back. He just laughed and shrugged his shoulders. Sometimes I felt ashamed for him when that beast of a woman was rude to him in front of other people. She had bought a bathing costume, red like that dress of hers, and she would put it on at midday to sunbathe, walking to and fro in front of the shed. She would keep it on even later, unless Ceresa took her by the arm and glared at her. Nora's skin was as creamy butter, but she never went bathing in the Po. When Damiano came along, or Zucca's son, she would stand laughing with them and showing herself. I can't understand what people see in women. 'You will,' Ceresa told me once. 'They'll appeal even to you.' But I haven't understood it yet.

Then Ceresa quarrelled with Damiano one day when I wasn't there. I heard people talking about it in the café next day. They had come to blows and were shouting so loudly that the tram-drivers on the other side of the river could hear them. That time I had a good look at Nora's face, without her knowing, wondering if she were angry, too, but she seemed more frightened than angry. Ceresa said nothing, but came fishing with me. That day there wasn't a single fish to pay him for his trouble, and he was so furious he took the basket and smashed it against one of the piles. Then he flung himself down in the bottom of the boat and told me to take him back home.

From then on I came only reluctantly to the landing-stage, unless Ceresa told me himself there was something he wanted me to do. There were some days when I sat there in the shed without saying a word, and Nora was nowhere to be seen. But it was worse still when Nora bustled round the kitchen or waited on the customers, because then I was always expecting her to say something. Then one day I went to look for my own little boat, the one I had made myself on the workbench in the shed, when Ceresa let me work there. I could not find it. Ceresa was sitting on the ground leaning against a post. I asked him if he knew where my boat was, but he said he had no idea. Then I ran into the kitchen and asked Nora. I heard her say, quite calmly, that she had burned it in the fire.

Ceresa asked me one day why I was not learning a trade. 'But I want to be a boatman, like you,' I replied.

'You're mad!' he exclaimed. 'Can't you see it's a devilish job? Tell your father he should get you into a factory. Tell him that. You'd even do better as a soldier than in this damned trade.'

It upset me, not for myself, for it made no difference to me, but for his sake. It was dreadful to think he no longer enjoyed the river. I wanted to tell him he should marry Nora; then he would be the boss and things would go better, but I didn't know what his reply might be. So I put my trousers on again and went home.

Nora realized she had really annoyed me, because next day she called me into the kitchen and made me talk. She asked me if I really loved boating so much. Wasn't I afraid of drowning? I replied that I liked it because it was Ceresa's trade. Then she asked if I could manage to take her out in a boat. 'Let's ask Ceresa if he'll let us go and see the weir,' she said. 'If it's fine tomorrow, we'll go then.'

Next day she put on her bathing costume and borrowed Ceresa's jacket. We took a picnic basket and Nora sat on the cushions. Ceresa laughed as he watched us start. Once we were past the bridge I started to row with long strokes.

Nora asked if we had far to go. I explained to her how
to use the oar, and showed her the way. She came over close
to me and we almost fell in the water. Women are all the
same. She went back and sat down, then asked me if I could
swim in deep water. She knew that nobody can swim
below the weir, and she asked me to stop by the mouth of
the Sangone where there is still water.

I tied the boat up to the bank, and she watched me as
I dived in. Then I swam in the Sangone and called to her
that the water was colder than in the Po. When I got back
to the boat and was just going to touch it, I saw Damiano
and a soldier coming to the bank. They were friends, but
the soldier I had never seen before. They came up to the
boat and started talking to Nora. I spoke to Damiano, but
I did not trust him. I jumped into the boat myself and sat
down.

Damiano made me furious, because I knew he could row
better than me, and if Nora asked him to take her up to the
weir I should look a fool. But Damiano and the soldier
sat down on the bank and began joking. Nora joined in,
and soon after she jumped on to the bank herself and said
she felt like taking a walk. The soldier put his hand on the
zipper of the jacket and said : 'What you really want is air.'
He was a man from Naples.

I stayed alone in the boat, thinking that if Ceresa got
to know about this there really would be trouble. Then I
got in the water again so that if anyone were to come along
they would not know it was Ceresa's boat. It was already
evening when Nora came back. She told me we shouldn't
tell Ceresa anything about having seen Damiano. I knew
that myself, anyway.

She tried to get me to take her out again, next day, this
time to the Mulini, but it wasn't my turn to come to the
landing-stage. I knew that, between Ceresa's insistence and
Nora looking at me as women do when they are furious, I

couldn't say no. So I went along towards evening and found her there. She had put on her skirt, but instead of a blouse she was still wearing the leather jacket. It was plain that now she had on her bathing costume under her skirt. She gave me a dirty look, but I stayed with Ceresa.

They were lovely, those September mornings, when the Po was swathed in mist and we waited for the sun to break through at any moment. Now there was always a job to be done at the forge or with a pot of pitch, and Nora was not about so early because she went to the market. Ceresa talked less than he used to do, but I gladly stayed with him because I knew he was dazed. He let me potter about in the shed as I liked, saying something to me now and again. And so I kept him company.

At last came the grape harvest, and one afternoon we picked bunches of them from the vines that covered the café and filled the bucket. Nora was there, too, and all three of us enjoyed a picnic, laughing as we ate them. Nora said we ought to be careful in case somebody stole them at night. Then, to show us where robbers might hide them, she zipped open the jacket. I had a glimpse of something white flecked with spots, and realized that under the jacket she was naked. She had left off her costume. Hastily she closed the zipper.

While we were having our picnic, there were two soldiers drinking beer at one of the little tables, and I fancied one of them was that friend of Damiano who had joked with Nora that day on the river bank. But how can one tell? They all look alike, and Nora had not paused when she took them their beer.

But an hour later I saw the same men again, laughing and talking with Nora. Ceresa had gone into the house. I saw Nora leaning over the table, and the soldier put his hand on the zipper as he had done that day, but this time he pulled it down. Nora still stood there, bending forward and laughing. I turned only when I heard Ceresa come to the door. He called me, but said nothing more.

A moment later I was alone on the bowling green, the little tables were empty, Ceresa and Nora had gone indoors. I stood still to hear if there was any shouting, but there was no sound or movement. All I was afraid of was that a customer might come along to hire a boat or bring one back, and I should have to call Ceresa. It was quiet among the trees and evening was coming on. I was cold. Beyond the trees I could hear the birds flying low. There was not even a car on the road. Everything seemed dead.

I was seized with fear, or shame; which, I don't know. I was still thinking of Nora's white skin. It seemed to me that evening was crying aloud, or listening to me shouting. Then the window opened. Ceresa leaned out and said: 'Pino, slip along home, now.' Then shut it quickly.

Next morning I went back with my heart in my mouth. I went along the top road without going down. The landing-stage was quiet between the trees. No one was there. I had to go on an errand to Dazio, but after lunch I decided: 'Ceresa ought to know that I wasn't to blame.'

I saw a great crowd of boats going and coming in front of the landing-stage; I saw two men in city clothes standing by a car at the entrance to the path. I knew I could not go past them so I walked round the field. People were crowding in and out of the shed, but Ceresa was not there. Then I came across Zucca's son. He told me that Ceresa had throttled Nora and thrown her into the Po.

I wanted to see him to tell him about that day by the Sangone, but they made us all move back, and when he came out the only sound was the noise of the car. Then my father told me the less I said about it the better, for me and everyone else.

First Love

Before I knew Nino it never struck me that the boys I ran shouting round the streets with were ragged and filthy. Indeed, I actually envied them for going barefoot. One of them could even walk over corn-stubble without being hurt, while my pale, city-dweller's feet cringed from the very thought of treading the cobbled streets.

They taught me a lot, but nothing of it interested Nino except a few swear-words. He lived in a little villa just outside the village and had several elder sisters who scared me stiff. I would stay just beyond the low, garden wall and peep through the railings, hoping Nino would be already coming down the steps. If he kept me waiting I would give a little hiss like a snake, softly at first but getting louder, as long as the dog didn't start barking. Then Nino would come running, because he was afraid of the dog, too.

It wouldn't have done at all to suggest to Nino any idea of going barefoot or playing with the others. I never told him so, but after I had been out with him a few times I felt ashamed of those old friends. Oddly enough, from his casual remarks I gathered he knew them all, the games they played and what they talked about. Indeed, he seemed one of us, except that his shirt and shorts were even cleaner than my own. He liked to stroll along side lanes with his hands in his pockets, peeping in at windows or between the tall grass at anyone who passed by, grinning every now and then.

We were both about thirteen or fourteen and that summer, to my surprise, I found I was beginning to dislike the urchins I used to play with; those of our own age were sloppy and stupid; any that seemed as lean and active as we were had already reached eighteen or so and didn't mix with us.

I can't clearly remember what Nino and I talked about in those early days. I know I once asked him how many sisters he had. 'None,' he replied.

'What? All those girls? Aren't they your sisters?'

'They're all like a mother to me,' he said, with his usual grimace. 'I doubt if they're really sisters, anyway.'

I told him that once I had gone hunting with a soldier on leave. I told him so many things, directly and indirectly, that one fine day Nino retorted: 'Rot!'

'What's that?' I exclaimed. 'I go hunting by myself, too. Any reason why I shouldn't?'

I took him down by the river one day. Some of the boys I played with in the mornings were fishing with creels and all soaked with water and mud. Nino stood aloof, giving me a faint smile when I called to him from the water, hoping for a glance of approval or a complimentary word. Once, when the blacksmith's son heaved out a heavy basket, creaking with the weight of fish in it, and called to him to catch hold of it, Nino moved aside and let it lie. They all yelled that he was 'dead on his feet'. I tried to make excuses for him, explaining that he was wearing a new coat, but Nino jeered back at them and shouted furiously that he had someone behind him who would soon put them in their proper place.

Nino stayed at home in the mornings, wandering round the house. The first time I went there to look for him, craning my neck up at his window, I saw a tall, handsome woman looking at me across the garden. She beckoned me to come closer, but I pretended not to notice and ran away. I was afraid Nino wouldn't speak to me any more, but it made no difference.

After that, I divided my time accordingly. Almost every morning I sneaked off to the goat pasture with the ragamuffins I had been friendly with at first. I stuffed them with exciting tales of the city – my own province – and extraordinary adventures that could happen on the trams or in lifts. Every now and then I would stop to chase a goat, peel a wand, or hunt grasshoppers. In the afternoons, instead of sheltering from the heat of the day in the hayloft or stable, as I used to do, I would go and look for Nino. I realized I was probably wasting my time and simply boring myself, yet every day I was there. When we returned from our casual stroll up the hill by the church or across the fields, I should have liked to go into the garden with him, to sit on those little chairs and risk being told off by his sisters, but the first time Nino asked me in I was too shy to accept.

After what happened at the fishing pool, I hinted that it would be best not to tell his family of our personal affairs. Nino laughed through his teeth and told me that if I was afraid the women in his home knew anything about those scruffy pals of mine, I needn't worry. His own friend was quite different.

One afternoon as we went past the open space behind the fertilizer store, I heard him laugh. Parked in the narrow street was a long, low car I had seen before. From the half-open door came the sound of many voices, suddenly dominated by a hearty laugh. Other laughs, louder still, followed the first. Nino peered forward through the stench of sulphur and manure and exclaimed: 'He's just coming out.'

125

Out came an old countryman who greeted us with a wink; then, flinging wide the door, he shouted: 'Toss 'em out.'

Out flew a heavy little sack that the old man caught in mid-air and put in the car. Then came another, and another.

'Give us a hand, young fellow,' said the old man, showing his gums. Nino leapt over the threshold and disappeared. I stayed by the car, trying to guess at the shadowy figures moving quickly about inside the place.

When the car was practically full and I was helping the old man readjust the bags, Nino appeared on the doorstep with a curly-haired man wearing a scarf round his neck, a red belt and Wellingtons. His sleeves were rolled up and he filled the doorway. Nino appeared at his elbow.

There was a smile in his voice as he said to Nino, and to me; 'So you've made friends, eh?' He gave me a wink and took my hand, but I broke away. He shook my forearm forcibly two or three times, then said: 'Nino, don't pick a quarrel with this one, for he's stronger than you.' Then he straightened up, looked round and said: 'Finished?'

He took out a cigarette and lit it, jumped into the car, called out 'So long' and was gone.

That evening Nino was full of excitement as he chatted to me. We went and sat on the low wall, but he couldn't stay still there. Yet his eyes hadn't the restless look they generally had and he answered my questions in a voice sparkling with gaiety.

Bruno worked as a chauffeur, but he was a real friend to Nino. He went to fetch them from the station the day they arrived, and all the way along the winding road over the hill to the villa Nino hardly bothered to answer anything his mother or sisters said, but talked to Bruno all the time, asking him about everything. Sometimes Bruno would ask him how the little heifers were getting on, meaning his sisters. (It was a saying with us : 'Silly as a heifer'.) There was only one thing that appealed to Bruno about those girls : the American cigarettes Nino brought him from them whenever he could – in their packets, of course, because the value depended on the packets.

Nino talked about all sorts of things that evening; the bathing pool at his home, that smelt even nicer than the meadows; how he wished he could get Bruno to bathe in it, too, so that he could still smell like a grown man, but clean; and especially about how he wanted to go out in the car with him, me too, touring the villages around the hills, having fun and learning to drive.

Bruno had promised to teach him, but there never seemed to be a chance. Bruno loved teasing everyone, pretending they were all stronger than he was. Then Nino gave me a pinch that almost took the skin off, and jumped clear. 'Let's see if you really are stronger,' he cried spitefully and picked up a stone.

If it had been one of those moments when we reached the gate of the villa and fell silent a moment before parting, I'd have asked Nino : 'Why do a thing like that?' But he'd never have said it, then. I couldn't understand why Nino had to spoil our friendly chat with such a spiteful remark. I couldn't go swimming in a lovely bathing pool, as he did, but I'd managed to grow stronger than he was.

'But there, he tells everyone they're stronger,' Nino went on, dropping the stone and coming over to me with a sly smile. But I couldn't trust myself to smile in return. 'So you like Bruno, eh?' he said. 'Careful. The heifers like him, too. My sisters, you know.'

'All of them?' I exclaimed.

'Yes, all of them,' Nino replied.

'But men choose just one woman,' I said.

'What a fool you are ! He can't exactly marry them.'

'But you told me he talked only with you.'

'That's because they never give him an answer. They're stupid.'

I went home feeling fed up, ashamed of my father's moustaches and the dirty, wine-stained oilcloth on the table where we ate our supper. My little sister kept on whining. I had never been in a car and was thinking how nice it would be to jump in one with Nino and Bruno. But it annoyed me that his sisters could be so stupid, and Nino himself so spiteful. Luckily I'd never told him that one night I'd dreamed about them.

Next morning I didn't want to go to the pasture with the other boys, as I usually did. Instead, I felt inclined to pass the time as Nino did, enjoying a good meal, then going for a bathe or sauntering round the house and turning up at noon. But by ten o'clock I was out in the courtyard wondering what to do next. On the slopes of the valley were low apple-trees, but I already knew them by heart. I strolled past the farm entrances, each with a pile of last year's wood outside it; I met the wife of a peasant farmer, carrying a bucket. She wore a yellow kerchief over her head and her sleeves were rolled up. I understood how it was that Nino could spend the whole morning without coming out to play, just watching those sisters of his walking about in the garden. It must be fine to live with them, if even the chauffeur found them desirable. All I had to look at was my mother and the servant, who both slaved like farm labourers, and my father only came home in the evening.

The peasant farmer's wife ran to the cowshed. I heard the cow bawling loudly, as if she was in pain, and I found myself in the doorway. The woman ran over to me. 'Get out. Get out!' she cried crossly, standing behind me so that I could not see past her. 'You shouldn't be watching. Go and call Pietro. Tell him it's time. Understand?'

Pietro was digging at the bottom of a field behind the

house. I came back with him. First he went into the kitchen and took a swig from a bottle, then we both ran to the shed. Again the old woman pushed me back. Pietro turned and muttered: 'Go and tell your mother we're getting a calf for her.'

I still hung around, trembling with fear at the animal groans that broke into the open air, followed by gurglings as if the creature was dying. Then came excited voices; the woman gave a sudden exclamation, followed by the splashing of water and the jingle of a chain. I thought about the shapeless mass of the cow's belly as I had seen it a day or two before.

Suddenly I thought of Nino and rushed off to find him. As I reached the villa, one of his sisters was coming out – the fair one with the dazzling white skin. I had watched her cycling past and thought how pretty she was. Now she laughed, rested her hand on my head and asked me what was the matter. I told her I was looking for Nino.

'Why?' she persisted.

'There's a new-born calf,' I stammered, red-faced. She looked at me, took her hand away and laughed aloud. 'Is it a pretty little thing?' she asked.

I didn't know what to say. She laughed again, turned away and called: 'Nino.' I heard an answering voice. She waved her hand, barely glancing at me, and went on her way, opening her parasol.

When Nino joined me – the dog was barking, rushing about and rattling his chain – I no longer wanted to take him to the cowshed. Again I felt ashamed of the filthy yard by our house. All I said was: 'Coming out?'

That morning we ended up by the river bank where the washerwomen were busy. Neither of us found anything to say. All at once I asked him: 'Ever seen a calf born? I did, this morning. It scared me.'

'Did it cry?' Nino asked.

'No, but its mother did. The cow, I mean.'

'Why didn't you call me?'

I felt annoyed, as I had done the day before. 'Silly ass!'
Nino cried in a fury. 'We could have seen how babies are
born. Have you ever seen how that happens?'

'Haven't you ever seen a young thing born?' I asked with
an air of importance.

Nino fell silent, looking down at the ground. The washerwomen were beating sheets against the stones. One of them
was a big, fat woman with bare arms. I could see her
armpits, and as she laughed with one of her friends her
whole body shook and quivered inside her shapeless dress.

'It's like seeing a horse pass dung,' Nino went on, his
voice a little unsteady. 'Only this is bigger. Did you really
see it?'

'Sure,' I replied.

'And you were born the same way,' Nino cried in a kind
of rage.

'Yes, I was,' I answered calmly.

Nino gave himself a punch in the face and dropped to
the ground. Standing beside him, I looked at him in some
embarrassment. I crouched down to confess the truth to
him, but just then he started laughing.

But his laugh sounded hollow. 'If you want to come out
in the car with us,' he said, 'Tell me what it's like.'

I stared at Nino. His eyes blazing, his lips trembling with
excitement. Softly he murmured: 'Have you seen your
mother?'

I stared at him in amazement and said: 'You silly fool!'

'Tell me, what did you see?'

'I saw the cow.'

'You haven't seen women?'

'No,' and I looked at the ground.

Nino's voice broke out, close to my ear, 'Then you don't
know what they do?'

130

I confessed that I hadn't even seen the calf.

Nino rolled over in the grass and rose to his feet. 'I know what they do,' he said. 'Blood comes out and they've got to pull the baby away from it.'

'Blood doesn't always come.'

'Yes it does. It always comes. That's why the women cry out.'

'No,' I said. 'Listen,' and I explained that once I had seen a cow as soon as her calf was born and there was no blood. The little calf was a bit wet, that's all.

'With women there's always blood,' Nino insisted. 'You don't know anything.'

In a hoarse voice he told me how things were with women. I didn't interrupt him. I just stood staring at the grass. When he had finished I asked: 'And your sisters too?'

'Yes. It's the same with them, too.'

That afternoon Bruno came to the village unexpectedly and invited us into the car with him. He had to take a demi-john of wine to the station and there was room for us. He settled us in the back seat to hold the demi-john and off we went. All the way along the road my heart was in my mouth. As the trees and fences and passers-by flashed past us I thought I was flying. I screwed up my eyes against the sun and watched Bruno's thick neck above his red kerchief, the jerky movements of his arm resting on the wheel. I was afraid that when we stopped the demi-john would fall.

Instead, all was well and I was the one to stagger, drenched in sweat, as I set foot on the ground. Bruno, talking in a loud voice, carried the demi-john into the left-luggage office, then took us to the station tavern. Timidly I sat down in the cool shade, trying to copy Nino who looked everyone straight in the face and laughed with Bruno, throwing his head back to look up at him.

Bruno called for beer and Nino wanted an ice. We had barely moistened our lips when Nino scowled and said slyly : 'Berto, tell Bruno you've seen a baby being made.'

Bruno looked sideways at me, with one eye. He put down his glass and pursed up his lips. 'Why you . . .' I burst out wildly to Nino.

Bruno wiped away the sweat from his face and turned to Nino. 'Better tell him you're learning to act like men. You should be, at your age. For the rest, that's for women to think of.'

'There was a calf born . . .' Nino said.

'A couple of asses, you mean,' Bruno interrupted him. 'Haven't you anything else to talk about?'

He wiped his face again and looked cross. We sat silent, our eyes cast down. Nino went on eating his ice, his head bent.

'Nino, did Clara give you the cigarettes?'

Clara was the fair-haired sister. 'She's hidden them,' Nino replied.

Bruno rolled one for himself and said casually : 'Would you like to come to the Robini's tomorrow? We'll be back by midday. You can come too, Berto.'

Nino said : 'Give me a smoke.'

I watched Bruno's huge hand rolling the cigarette, not daring to ask for one myself. 'Coming tomorrow, Nino?' I said instead. Nino gave Bruno a sly look and asked softly : 'Shall we stop by the little wall?'

Bruno nodded, holding his cigarette out to him. I could not understand why Nino looked so pale. I saw his hand trembling as he lit his cigarette from Bruno's. 'Have a drink of wine,' Bruno said. 'Ice cream's for weaklings.' I knew Nino didn't like red wine, yet I watched him hold out his glass and lift it slowly to his lips. He swallowed it all.

'Fine,' Bruno exclaimed. 'While you're in town, this

winter, you won't get wine like this. You'll get thin, in town. What about you, Berto? Got a girl-friend yet?'

I felt embarrassed, but managed to reply: 'There's no time for that: we're at school all the winter.'

'You have a girl in the summer, then?'

'I . . . no.'

Bruno laughed aloud. 'Bravo! You'll be seeing Nino this winter?'

'This year we shall, shan't we?' I asked Nino abruptly.

'You be careful! Nino takes fencing lessons and might run you through,' Bruno winked at me.

Nino said nothing. He drank another glass, barely listening to us. His eyes were fixed on the leather strap Bruno wore round his square wrist, and he suddenly asked what it was for.

'To bash in the face of any cheeky blighter,' Bruno explained. 'You give him a sideways blow, overhand, so as not to hurt your fingers, and it acts like a boxing glove. One night at Spigno there was a fellow who walked by the car – I was parked by the station – and he spat into it. Just spat and ran away. You must never put up with spitting, because a man who spits is afraid. I shot after him and split open his face. Like this. See how it works?'

Nino coughed over his cigarette, without taking his eyes from Bruno's fierce face. Smoking didn't worry him at all, as I knew already from the other times we had smoked together behind the church, so it must be the wine that was upsetting him. Or perhaps the argument he'd had with Bruno. Why did Bruno call his sister by her christian name?

'When your mother and sisters take that trip to Acqui they're talking about, I'll show you the market-place where I stopped a mad dog by pushing the leather in his mouth. See the marks of his teeth?'

'I'm not coming to Acqui with you,' said Nino.

Bruno started laughing: 'Berto, finish your drink. Tomorrow, then.'

We went to the Robini's, speeding all the way. Every time we rounded a curve, Bruno turned towards me and whistled through his teeth. Nino, sitting beside him, kept his chin against his chest as if someone had hit him. Two or three times his eyes wandered over the hills or up into the sky, and he gave a sudden start as though he had just woken up.

'The land is very dry, this year,' I remarked in a resigned tone of voice, as my father did.

This time Bruno did not turn towards me. Instead, he swung round into a narrow side-track between steep banks covered with flowers. For five minutes our faces were lashed by twigs. Then we came to a halt half-way up a hillside, near a little bridge whose walls overhung a rocky gorge. Bruno jumped out and said: 'You wait here. Look after the car.'

He switched off the engine and took out the key. 'Don't touch anything, and it won't move. Cheer up, Nino.' He gave us each a cigarette and lit it for us. 'If anybody comes up this way, anyone at all, sound the horn. Understand? If all goes well I'll let you drive, Nino. You, too, Berto. But keep a good look out. Anyone at all, remember.' He went up a little steep path and disappeared behind the banks.

The sun was blazing down, now. Shaded by the high banks we could watch a long stretch of the track up the hill. No one could turn into it from the main road without our seeing them. I had never been up here before, but evidently Nino had. There he sat at the wheel, never bothering to glance at the wide views spread out before our eyes, but smoking as a man does, puffing away without looking down at his cigarette.

'Will Bruno be away long?' I asked.

Nino did not answer. He jumped down and walked

around the car, scrutinizing the headlamps and the dusty tyres. From the walls of the bridge he looked down at the river bed, now dry. Only when the autumn rains came would it fill again and become a raging torrent masked with foam. Now there were only knotted roots. It looked tempting to climb down by them, but for the risk of snakes. I threw away my cigarette stub, then tried to put it out by spitting at it. Nino made no move.

'Let me sit there a bit, too,' I said, turning towards him.

Nino looked at me, his eyes narrowing as they did when he felt spiteful. 'Know where he's gone?' he asked.

I shrugged my shoulders, and at that moment a dog started barking, not far away.

'See?' said Nino. 'That means he's just got to the house where the woman is. He's gone to find Martino's wife or daughter. They're expecting him. They'll tie up the dog and go to bed together.'

'But it's broad daylight!' I exclaimed.

Now Nino gave a shrug. 'They'll get on the bed as quick as they can,' he went on. 'They may be there an hour,' and he laughed, 'if nobody comes.'

'And where's Martino?'

'He's gone to the station. I heard about it yesterday.'

'And if he comes back?'

'If he comes, it's our job to sound the horn.'

I was not convinced. 'Did Bruno tell you about it?'

Nino gave me a dirty look and tossed away his cigarette end.

'I don't believe it,' I persisted. 'It would take too long. Bruno's got other things to think of. And he's got to drive the car, too.'

'What about it?'

'. . . He'd be too exhausted . . .' I faltered.

'Bruno's strong,' Nino exclaimed in a fury. 'But you'll see.'

'What?'

'You'll see.'

The narrow track still lay deserted in the hot sunshine. The very leaves before my eyes were trembling in the heat. Or perhaps it was that my heart was beating wildly. The village and my home seemed so remote from the quiet solitude around us, and from the thoughts in my mind. If only Nino didn't sound so spiteful! I thought about Clara, back in the villa and knowing nothing of what we were doing. She was a woman, too. Unsteadily I sat down on the running board of the car.

'I don't believe you,' I said abruptly. 'The Martino women attend church regularly.'

'All women go to church. They get married in church. Didn't you know? And when a couple marry it's so that they can go to bed together, isn't it?'

'I just don't believe it,' I said. 'Bruno is a good man, like us.'

'Know what I'll do to him?'

'What?'

'You'll see.'

I jumped into the car and sat beside Nino. He gave me a sly look and whistled to himself. 'At this very minute they're kissing and cuddling each other,' he said through his clenched teeth.

'Nino,' I cried. 'What'll we do if Martino comes back? He'll be sure to find him there . . .'

'He won't come back,' Nino replied. 'Is that someone coming?' He turned and surveyed the track, the main road and the whole plain. We strained our ears. There was nobody.

'Now they've stripped off their clothes,' Nino went on, and his face was pale.

'But . . .' I stammered.

'Quick, now,' Nino cried, and pressed the horn.

In response came a furious barking from the dog. In the moment that followed it semed to me that the whole woodland was in an uproar. I tried to stop Nino's hand, but already the raucous blare of the horn, like the shout of a madman, was re-echoing from the hills.

When Bruno came bounding down the path, we were hiding in the long grass behind the tree-trunks, where Nino had dragged me. Bruno looked all around, especially at the track from the main road, his red belt still dangling from his hand. He strapped it around his trousers, still peering in every direction. Then, keeping his voice low, he called : 'Nino !' Nino gripped my arm.

Bruno had jumped in the car and was scrutinizing the main road far below. His lips were moving. His hair was all over the place and his face looked as if he had just held it under the pump. He got down from the car and went over to the tree, turned his back and stood with his legs wide apart. A moment later we heard him passing water. Nino stifled a giggle.

Then Bruno came over in our direction, looking up into the air and buttoning his trousers. Suddenly he leaned forward and leapt between the branches. Nino tried to flee, but he gripped him by the leg and brought him down. I had jumped to my feet and stood there watching. Without saying a word, Bruno gripped Nino's wrists in one hand and held him up like a rabbit, screeching and kicking. With the other hand he thrashed his bottom. His lips were tight together, and every blow made Nino scream. For a moment he looked at me without seeing me, and I fled down the track. The noise of a scuffle continued, then Bruno appeared, carrying Nino under his arm and throwing him into the car. To me he shouted roughtly. 'Get in. We're going back.'

All the way back, Nino never said a word, held tight against Bruno's side. The wind against my face felt as cold as if I'd had a fever. In front of the villa, Bruno stopped. He watched me get out, and for a moment I thought he was laughing. Nino raised his head, pushed my arm aside and got out unsteadily. He spat on the ground and went off through the garden, staggering as he walked.

Next day I didn't dare to call for Nino because, when I reached the gate, I saw two of his sisters – the dark ones – sitting in the garden, stretching out their legs in the sunshine. One of them was reading.

I was playing around, towards evening, when Clara rode up on her bicycle and jumped off as she came up to me. 'Where did you boys go, yesterday?' she asked me. 'What did Bruno do to Nino? Where did you go? Nino's had to stay in bed all day. What did you do to Bruno?'

'Where's Bruno?' I said.

Clara gave me a keen look and walked on towards the gate, pushing her bicycle. 'I don't know where Bruno is,' she went on. 'I don't even know him. Still, he must have done something, because Nino won't tell me about it. Did you go to the Robini's?'

'Something went wrong with the car,' I said.

'What were you doing at the Robini's?'

'Nothing. We were learning to drive.'

By now we were inside the garden, but the wicker chairs under the big umbrella were empty. The gravel scrunched under out feet. 'Did you go there to find somebody?' she asked.

'Oh, no.'

Clara said more seriously, 'Nino's in bed. Would you like to come and see him?'

'Oh, no. I'll come and call for him tomorrow. It's late, now,' I said, coming to a halt.

' How's the calf?' Clara asked with a smile.

'What calf?'

138

'The one born the other day. Is it yours?'

I nodded in reply. Clara leaned the bicycle against the wall and went on up the steps. 'So long, for now, little calf,' she called to me as she turned away. I noticed how tall she was.

For several days after that Nino did not come out at all. I walked up and down in front of the villa, hoping to catch sight of someone or other. It was the time of year, early in August, when there's nothing much to do in the country; the apples and early plums are finished in July and the grape harvest doesn't start till September. While I was waiting for Nino to come back to me, there seemed no point in joining up with my former friends again, so I wandered aimlessly round the lanes all by myself. Still, it's a good thing to be alone sometimes when you have something on your mind, or when you've just had a glimpse of Clara through the garden railings. Still, the days seemed awfully long.

I remember there were frightful thunderstorms on some of those afternoons and the sky was cold and black, though we had no hail. They terrified my mother and the cattle in the sheds, but I rather liked them because the evenings were cool and next morning there were pools of water, with piles of leaves strewn on the ground. I thought about Clara and her sisters, wondering whether the lightning had frightened them.

At last I saw Nino again, but he hadn't much to say. Once or twice I couldn't help laughing to see how gingerly he sat down on the garden wall. He looked slyly at me, and it seemed as if we'd got back to the old days when we strolled about together with hardly a word. One day he brought along a whole packet of fine cigarettes with arabic printing on the packet. The one I had was scented and made me feel sick. One morning at the river where we swam I saw him strolling casually along with his jacket over

his shoulder. He sat on the bank and started smoking.
Immediately all the other boys swarmed around him and
he gave two or three of them a cigarette. He spat in the
water and asked lightly : 'Have any of you seen that
chauffeur lately, the one from the *Ca' Nere*?'

He discussed it with the fair-haired fellow from the
Mulini, the one whose brother was a porter at the station,
and decided that, if he didn't come before, Bruno would
have to come through the village for the festival of the
August Madonna, to load up the flour. Nino remarked
calmly : 'That Martino fellow's looking for him, to skin
him alive.'

The blacksmith's son remarked that his cigarette tasted
of honey, yet it was strong. We four boys strolled home
together. The blacksmith's boy already wore long trousers
down to his bare ankles, and was always scratching his
chest under his shirt. In two or three days Nino was on such
good terms that they were giggling and scrapping like old
friends.

Then Nino asked me one day : 'Didn't Bruno do anything
to you, that time?'

'Who was it sounded the horn?' I retorted.

Nino looked sideways at me as we walked along – and
his eyes were really shifty in those days. 'Berto,' he said,
'you're a fool.'

By now there were several afternoons when I did not
see him at all. He went about with one of the other boys;
they even went fishing, and I knew that once Nino brought
along a packet of candied peaches as well as the cigarettes.
On that ocasion I told him : 'Take care they don't do you
an injury. They only come with you for what you bring
them.' But Nino replied that he knew that, too.

On the evening of the bonfire for the Madonna, Nino
kept out of sight and his sisters did not come out into the
garden to watch the fires dotted all over the hills. It was

the first time I ever spent that festival alone and uneasy. Next day a boy told me that Nino had gone with the others to make a bonfire in the Mulini's field, and when he saw a chance he had pushed the blacksmith's son right into the fire. Now that lad was out to catch Nino and threatening to slaughter him.

Next time I went by the villa, Nino sent the gardener's wife out to call me in. He begged me to go and fetch Bruno for him. The '*Ca' Nere*' was a long way off, but I went there and left word at the garage that Bruno was wanted at the villa. As I went back into the garden again, stones and lumps of earth rained against my back. The blacksmith's son and the other boys were on the watch in case Nino ever came out.

An hour or so later, Bruno arrived, very smart in his rubber Wellingtons and that hideous kerchief of his. I stopped him by the gate for a minute of two, hoping the boys would start pelting us again. Bruno believed the message was about that trip to Acqui. He gave Nino a clout, but Nino only flushed, went over close to him and asked if he'd like to make it up. Bruno seemed in no hurry to reply, and gave a casual look at the end of the garden. Then he burst out laughing and said: 'All right. What d'you want?'

That moment a clod of earth hit Nino on the back. He jumped aside, clutched at Bruno's fist and exclaimed: 'Those louts down there. Let' em have it, Bruno!' When Bruno knew who they were and why they were there, he half-turned to look at them and shouted at us: 'You kids! You're worse than women, you really are! And those fellows down there don't care, because they're all in it together.'

Just then Clara came out, spoke to Bruno and started talking about that trip to Acqui. 'Come over here if you want to see something,' Nino said to me and I went across

141

the garden, half-turning to look at Clara who was leaning on the gate, listening to Bruno.

The next moment a shower of stones hit Bruno in the face and Clara screamed. We ran over. Already Bruno had grabbed two of the band, one of them the blacksmith's son, and was kicking them off. I came to a halt by the gate, quivering with excitement and clenching my fists as Clara watched me. If those wretches wanted any more, I was ready. Bruno came back laughing, said good-bye to Clara and gave Nino another box on the ear. We were all a bit worked up.

We had some glorious August days after that and Nino often asked me into the garden when we came back from some excursion or other. (The dog was now tied up at the back of the villa.) Once we sat under the big sunshade and had a picnic of bread and jam. Nino, lounging in a deck chair, told me he always had jam to eat, even in town; this winter he'd take me to fencing class with him and I'd see what fun it was. Another year he'd be going to the sea in July; if I'd like to come too, we'd go in a boat together. We'd have to wear sandals, and before we went there I'd have to be able to swim.

'Aren't your sisters going to get married?' I asked him.

'One's married,' he told me, 'but she's not here. A year or so ago, Clara was going to be married, but they quarrelled.'

'And your mother?' His mother was one of the brunettes whom I had taken for one of his sisters. I couldn't believe it.

'Nothing but women in our house,' Nino said. 'At least if Clara went away . . .'

It was fine to be with Nino like this. He never said anything spiteful to me now. If we went for another run in the car with Bruno round the countryside, there was no quarrelling. Clara sent him cigarettes by us, and he stuffed them in his pocket with a laugh.

The only thing we had to worry about was the blacksmith's son. His hair was still singed and he watched us fiercely, from a distance, his mouth twisted in a snarl.

But one day he suddenly appeared at the church porch as we were passing by, and came over to us. He asked Nino for a cigarette. Nino shrugged his shoulders. Then he said: 'If you give me one, I'll tell you something that'll make you give me a whole packet.'

'Go on, give him one,' I whispered to Nino. 'Then you'll be friends again.'

But Nino hadn't any. The other laughed. 'It doesn't matter. Come round to the Orchard and I'll show you something worth seeing.'

'D'you take us for a couple of fools?' Nino answered.

The blacksmith's son put his yellow teeth close to Nino's ear and whispered breathily. Nino turned pale and jumped back; looked at me, then at him and stammered: 'Word of honour?'

'What is it?' I asked.

'Let's go,' Nino said.

The Orchard was a dairy-farm on the slope of the hill behind the villa. Between the villa and the first cleft in the rocky ground stretched a large vineyard, almost flat, shut in by a reed-bed and a patch of barren land. We reached the reeds and jumped through them, pushing our way between the rows. Silently I picked up a knotted stump in case the blacksmith's son might be leading us into an ambush.

'Seen Bruno today?' I asked suddenly, to give Nino a hint, and the other fellow, too.

Nino's lips were quivering and he made no reply. He and his companion were making their way towards the Red Shack, a deserted hut shut in by trees, at the far end of the rows. I had played at soldiers there, a year ago.

'Quiet,' Nina murmured when we were fairly close to it. 'You stop where you are. You, Berto, keep him with you.' Then he went forward and stopped on the bare patch by the entrance. The wooden door was shut. Walking lightly, Nino went round the corner and raised himself on tiptoe by the window.

My companion gave a low laugh. 'D'you want to know what it is?' he said. 'Come and see.'

So we went forward, too, and rejoined Nino, who was supporting himself on the board that held the window-frame and staring through the filthy glass. I tried to look in, too, but saw nothing because my eyes were still dazzled by the sunshine. But something was moving inside, in the darkness.

Then I could make out a white body lying at full length and a man just breaking away from it; a man with a red kerchief. It was Bruno, and the woman was Clara. There was a kind of golden sheen over her bare body. The dusty panes masked the scene in a kind of mist.

'She's white, isn't she?' the smith's son whispered.

Nino jumped back. 'Come away,' he said softly, between his teeth. 'Come away.' I felt his nails digging into my back. The smith's son aimed a kick at him. 'If you don't come, I'll call Bruno,' Nino hissed furiously. The other tore himself away, giving Nino a dirty grin, and backed slowly away over the empty patch of ground. They stared at each other a moment, then Nino ran at him and the other fled.

I ran, too, desperately, still clutching my stump of wood. By now, Nino had caught up with him and brought him to the ground. They were rolling over and over, biting each other. I threw myself into the fight, kicking and hitting out at those patched trousers, that filthy shirt and those yellow teeth, thrashing him as if I thought Clara could see me.

At last the blacksmith's son started crying and howling, and I broke away. Even Nino was exhausted. We left our enemy lying in a furrow and ran away. I think Nino had the same idea in mind as I had, because, weary and exhausted as he was, he rushed off like a horse, trying to outdistance me. Suddenly I stopped and let him go ahead. That way we avoided saying anything.

From a distance I watched him turn the corner of the villa. I stayed behind by myself, on a heap of gravel by the roadside. Only when I was nearly home did I notice that my neck was covered with blood, but to me it didn't matter; I went in through the farmyard and flung myself down on the hay. It was already dark when I struggled lazily to my feet and rubbed the dried blood from my cheeks – as if the drops had been tears – wondering whether all the sisters were like Clara.

Next day I heard that Nino had a broken arm. I didn't dare to go to the villa for fear they might have seen us. For many nights after that I stayed awake hour after hour, clutching my pillow and screwing up my eyes. One night, when there was a moon, if I hadn't been too scared I would have got up and gone to the hut to see if there were any traces. I tried to go next morning, but a man was working in the vineyard and I didn't dare go there.

Now I hardly ever went outside our own yard, for fear of having stones or lumps of earth thrown at me, but then the other boys called for me to go fishing with them – they needed my net. Since Nino had a broken arm, the smith's son didn't dare say a word. But one day, when we were talking in the hayloft with the blond fellow from Mulini's, he asked me if Nino's sister was fair, too. I felt ashamed afterwards, but on the spur of the moment I couldn't stop myself from talking. Yet my heart was in my mouth as I spoke and suddenly I felt despairing and hopeless, just as when I was a little boy sitting naked on a chair in the kitchen, watching the water being poured into my bath. Then I stopped talking, and the blond chap fell silent, too.

At last, one morning I saw Bruno cycling by; he stopped and called to me: 'Have you quarrelled with Nino?' Now he was wearing a black neckerchief and a shirt with pockets. He told me that Nino had asked him, only yesterday, to find me and tell me to come and see him. That story he'd told about falling from a rotten tree hadn't convinced anybody. Those scratches on his face were the work of a boy. 'And if I didn't recognize your hand in it, I'd say a girl made them,' he concluded.

I stared at him incredulously. 'You go and see him,' he went on. 'No need for men to be at loggerheads. Nino wants you. He'll tell you how babies are born.'

'But have you been to see him?' I asked him with some hesitation.

'Sure. We're friends, aren't we? He's in fine form, that lad. A broken arm will set in a couple of weeks, and he wants to come out in the car with me.'

Bruno took out a cigarette, lit it, blew out a puff of smoke and straightened up his bicycle.

'What do his sisters say about it?' I asked.

'Oh, they couldn't care less, one way or the other,' Bruno replied, 'and the mother is worse than any of them. The only one who bothers about him at all is the blonde one.' He rode away down the road and I followed him with my eyes. I felt in a daze, but deep down I was happy.

Wedding Trip

Now that I, shattered and full of remorse, have learned how foolish it is to reject reality for the sake of idle fancies, how presumptuous to receive when one has nothing to give in return, now – Cilia is dead. Though I am resigned to my present life of drudgery and ignominy, I sometimes think how gladly I would adapt myself to her ways, if only those days could return. But perhaps that is just another of my fancies. I treated Cilia badly when I was young, when nothing should have made me irritable; no doubt I should have gone on ill-treating her, out of bitterness and the disquiet of an unhappy conscience. For instance, I am still not sure after all these years, whether I really loved her. Certainly I mourn for her; I find her in the background of my inmost thoughts; never a day passes in which I do not shrink painfully away from my memories of those two years, and I despise myself because I let her die. I grieve for her youth, even more for my own loneliness, but – and this is what really counts – did I truly love her? Not, at any rate, with the sincere, steady love a man should have for his wife.

The fact is, I owed her too much, and all I gave her in return was a blind suspicion of her motives. As it happens, I am by nature superficial and did not probe more deeply into such dark waters. At the time I was content to treat the matter with my instinctive diffidence and refused to give weight or substance to certain sordid thoughts that, had they taken root in my mind, would have sickened me of the whole affair. However, several times I did ask myself: ' And why did Cilia marry me?' I do not know whether it was due to a sense of my own importance, or to profound ineptitude, but the fact remains that it puzzled me.

There was no doubt that Cilia married me, not I her. Oh! Those depressing evenings I endured in her company – wandering restlessly through the streets, squeezing her arm, pretending to be free and easy, suggesting as a joke that we should jump in the river together. Such ideas didn't bother me – I was used to them – but they upset her, made her anxious to help me; so much so that she offered me, out of her wages as a shop-assistant, a little money to live on while I looked for a better job. I did not want money. I told her that to be with her in the evenings was enough for me, as long as she didn't go away and take a job somewhere else. So we drifted along. I began to tell myself, sentimentally, that what I needed was someone nice to live with; I spent too much time roaming the streets; a loving wife would know how to contrive a little home for me, and just by going into it I should be happy again, no matter how weary and miserable the day had made me.

I tried to tell myself that even alone I managed to muddle along quite well, but I knew this was no argument. ' Two people together can help each other,' said Cilia, ' and take care of one another. If they're a little in love, George, that's enough.' I was tired and disheartened, those evenings; Cilia was a dear and very much in earnest, with the fine coat she had made herself and her little broken handbag. Why not give her the joy she wanted? What other girl would suit me better? She knew what it was to work hard and be short of money; she was an orphan, of working-class parents; I was sure that she was more eager and sincere than I.

On impulse I told her that if she would accept me, uncouth and lazy as I was, I would marry her. I felt content, soothed by the warmth of my good deed and proud to discover I had that much courage. I said to Cilia: ' I'll teach you French!' She responded with a smile in her gentle eyes as she clung tightly to my arm.

2

In those days I thought I was sincere, and once again I explained to Cilia how poor I was. I warned her that I hardly ever had a full day's work and didn't know what it was to get a pay-packet. The college where I taught French paid me by the hour. One day I told her that if she wanted to get on in the world she ought to look for some other man. Cilia looked troubled and offered to keep on with her job. ' You know very well that isn't what I want,' I muttered. Having settled things thus, we married.

It made no particular difference to my life. Already, in the past, Cilia had sometimes spent evenings with me in my room. Lovemaking was no novelty. We took two furnished rooms; the bedroom had a wide, sunny window, and there we placed the little table with my books.

Cilia, though, became a different woman. I, for my part, had been afraid that, once married, she would grow vulgar and slovenly – as I imagined her mother had been – but instead I found her more particular, more considerate towards me. She was always clean and neat, and kept everything in perfect order. Even the simple meals she prepared for me in the kitchen had the cordiality and solace of those

hands and that smile. Her smile, especially, was trans-
figured. It was no longer the half-timid, half-teasing smile
of a shop-girl on the spree, but the gentle flowering of an
inner joy, utterly content and eager to please, a serene light
on her thin young face. I felt a twinge of jealousy at this
sign of a happiness I did not always share. 'She's married
me and she's enjoying it,' I thought.

Only when I woke up in the morning was my heart at
peace. I would turn my head against hers in our warm bed
and lie close beside her as she slept (or was pretending to),
my breath ruffling her hair. Then Cilia, with a drowsy
smile, would put her arms around me. How different from
the days when I woke alone, cold and disheartened, to stare
at the first gleam of dawn!

Cilia loved me. Once she was out of bed, she found fresh
joys in everything she did as she moved around our room,
dressing herself, opening the windows, stealing a cautious
glance at me. If I settled myself at the little table, she
walked quietly so as not to disturb me; if I went out, her
eyes followed me to the door; when I came home she
sprang up quickly to greet me.

There were days when I did not want to go home at all.
It irritated me to think I should inevitably find her there,
waiting for me, even though she learned to pretend she took
no special interest; I should sit beside her, tell her more or
less the same things, or probably nothing at all. We should
look at one another with distaste and a smile. It would be
the same tomorrow and the next day, and always. Such
thoughts entrapped me whenever the day was foggy and
the sun looked grey. If, on the other hand, there was a
lovely day when the air was clear and the sun blazed down
on my head, or a perfume in the wind enfolded and en-
raptured me, I would linger in the streets, wishing that I
still lived alone, free to stroll around till midnight and get a

meal of some sort at the pub on the corner of the street. I had always been a lonely man, and it seemed to me to count for a great deal that I was not unfaithful to Cilia.

She, waiting for me at home, began to take in sewing, to earn a little. A neighbour gave her work, a certain Amalia, a woman of thirty or so, who once invited us to dinner. She lived alone in the room below ours, and gradually fell into the habit of bringing the work upstairs to Cilia so that they could pass the afternoon together. Her face was disfigured by a frightful scar – when she was a little girl she had pulled a boiling saucepan down on her head. Her two sorrowful, timid eyes, full of longing, flinched away when anyone looked at her, as if their humility could excuse the distortion of her features. She was a good girl. I remarked to Cilia that Amalia seemed to me like her elder sister. One day, for a joke, I said: ' If I should run away and leave you, one fine day, would you go and live with her?' ' She's had such bad luck all her life. I wouldn't mind if you wanted to make love to her!' Cilia teased me. Amalia called me 'Sir' and was shy in my presence. Cilia thought this was madly funny. I found it rather flattering.

3

It was a bad thing for me that I regarded my scanty intellectual attainments as a substitute for a regular trade. It lay at the root of so many of my wrong ideas and evil actions. But my education could have proved a good means of communion with Cilia, if only I had been more consistent. Cilia was very quick, anxious to learn everything I knew myself because, loving me so much, she could not bear to feel unworthy of me. She wanted to understand my every thought. And – who knows? – if I could have given her this simple pleasure I might have learned, in the quiet intimacy of our joint occupation, what a fine person she really was, how real and beautiful our life together, and perhaps Cilia would still be alive at my side, with her lovely smile that in two years I froze from her lips.

I started off enthusiastically, as I always do. Cilia's education consisted of a few back numbers of serial novels, the news in the daily papers, and a hard, precocious experience of life itself. What was I to teach her? She very much wanted to learn French and indeed, Heaven knows how, she managed to piece together scraps of it by searching through my dictionaries when she was left alone at home. But I aspired to something better than that and wanted to teach her to read properly, to appreciate the finest books. I kept a few of them – my treasures – on the little table. I tried to explain to her the finer points of novels and poems, and Cilia did her best to follow me. No-one excels me in recognising the beauty, the 'rightness' of a thought or a story, and explaining it in glowing terms. I put a great deal of effort into making her feel the freshness of ancient pages, the truth of sentiments expressed long before she and I were born, how varied, how glorious, life had been for so many many men at so many different periods. Cilia would listen with close attention, asking questions that I often found embarrassing. Sometimes as we strolled in the streets or sat eating our supper in silence, she would tell me in her candid voice of certain doubts she had, and once when I replied without conviction or with impatience – I don't remember which – she burst out laughing.

I remember that my first present to her, as her husband, was a book, *The Daughter of the Sea*. I gave it to her a month after our wedding, when we started reading lessons. Until then I had not bought her anything – nothing for the house, no new clothes – because we were too poor. Cilia was delighted and made a new cover for the book, but she never read it.

Now and then, when we had managed to save enough, we went to a cinema, and there Cilia really enjoyed herself. An additional attraction, for her, was that she could snuggle up close to me, and now and then ask me for explanations that she could understand. She never let Amalia come to the cinema with us, though one day the poor girl asked if she could. She explained to me that we got to know each other best of all in a cinema, and in that blessed darkness we had to be alone together.

Amalia came to our place more and more often. This, and my well-deserved disappointments, soon made me first neglect our reading lessons, and finally stop them altogether. Then, if I was in a good mood, I amused myself by joking with the two girls, and Amalia lost a little of her shyness. One evening, as I came home very late from the college with my nerves on edge, she came and stared me full in the face, with a gleam of reproof and suspicion in her timid glance. I felt more disgusted than ever by the frightful scar on her face, and spitefully I tried to make out what her features had been before they were destroyed. I remarked to Cilia, when we were alone, that Amalia, as a child must have been very like her.

' Poor thing,' said Cilia. ' She spends every penny she earns trying to get cured. She hopes that then she'll find a husband.'

' But don't all women know how to get a husband?'

' I've already found mine,' Cilia smiled.

' Suppose what happened to Amalia had happened to you?' I sneered.

Cilia came close to me. ' Wouldn't you want me any more?'

' No.'

153

'But what's upset you this evening? Don't you like Amalia to come up here? She gives me work and helps me ....'

What had got into me – and I couldn't get rid of it – was the thought that Cilia was just another Amalia. I felt disgusted and furious with both of them. My eyes were hard as I stared at Cilia, and the tender look she gave me only made me pity her, irritating me still more. On my way home I had met a husband with two dirty brats clinging round his neck, and behind him a thin worn-out little woman, his wife. I imagined what Cilia would look like when she was old and ugly, and the thought clutched me by the throat.

Outside, the stars were shining. Cilia looked at me in silence. 'I'm going for a walk,' I told her with a bitter smile, and I went out.

4

I had no friends and I realised, now and then, that Cilia was my whole life. As I walked the streets I thought about us and felt troubled that I did not earn enough to repay her by keeping her in comfort, so that I needn't feel ashamed when I went home. I never wasted a penny – I did not even smoke – and, proud of that, I considered my thoughts were at least my own. But what could I make of those thoughts? On my way home I looked at people and wondered how so many of them had managed to succeed in life. Desperately I longed for changes, for something fresh and exciting.

I used to hang around the railway station, thrilled by the smoke and the bustle. For me, good fortune has always meant adventure in far-away places – a liner crossing the ocean, arrival at some exotic port, the clang of metal, shrill, foreign voices – I dreamed of it all the time. One evening I stopped short, terrified by the sudden realisation that if I didn't hurry up and travel somewhere with Cilia while she was still young and in love with me, I should never go at all. A fading wife and a squalling child would, for ever, prevent me. ' If only we really had money,' I thought again. ' You can do anything with money.'

' Good fortune must be deserved,' I told myself. ' Shoulder every load that life may bring. I am married but I do not want a child. Is that why I'm so wretched? Should I be luckier if I had a son?'

To live always wrapped up in oneself is a depressing thing, because a brain that is habitually secretive does not hesitate to follow incredibly stupid trains of thought that mortify the man who thinks them. This was the only origin of the doubts that plagued me.

Sometimes my longing for far-away places filled my mind even in bed. If, on a still and windless night, I suddenly caught the wild sound of a train whistle in the distance, I would start up from Cilia's side with all my dreams re-awakened.

One afternoon, when I was passing the station without even stopping, a face I knew suddenly appeared in front of me and gave a cry of greeting. Malagigi: I hadn't seen him for ten years. We shook hands and stood there exchanging courtesies. He was no longer the ugly, spiteful ink-spotted little devil I knew at school, always playing jokes in the lavatory, but I recognised that grin of his at once. ' Malagigi! Still alive, then?'

' Alive, and a qualified accountant.' His voice had changed. It was a man speaking to me now.

' Are you off somewhere, too?' he asked. ' Guess where I'm going!' As he spoke he picked up a fine leather suit-

case that toned perfectly with his smart new raincoat and
the elegance of his tie. Gripping my wrist he went on:
' Come to the train with me. I'm going to Genoa.'

' I'm in a hurry.'

' Then I leave for China!'

' No!'

' It's true. Can't a man go to China? What have you got
against China? Instead of talking like that, wish me luck!
Perhaps I may stay out there.'

' But what's your job?'

' I'm going to China. Come and see me off.'

' No, I really can't spare the time.'

' Then come and have coffee with me, to say goodbye.
You're the last man I shall talk to, here.'

We had coffee there in the station, at the counter, while
Malagigi, full of excitement, told me in fits and starts all
about himself and his prospects. He was not married. He'd
fathered a baby, but luckily it died. He had left school after
I did, without finishing. He thought of me once, when he
had to take an exam a second time. He'd gained his
education in the battle of life. Now all the big firms had
offered him a job. And he spoke four languages. And they
were sending him to China.

I said again that I was in a hurry, (though it was not
true), and managed to get away from him, feeling crushed
and overwhelmed. I reached home still upset by the chance
meeting, my thoughts in a turmoil. How could he rise from
such a drab boyhood to the audacious height of a future
like that? Not that I envied Malagigi, or even liked him;
but to see, unexpectedly superimposed on his grey background, which had been mine, too, his present colourful
and assured existence, such as I could glimpse only in
dreams, was torment to me.

Our room was empty, because now Cilia often went downstairs to work in our neighbour's room. I stayed there a while, brooding in the soft darkness lit only by the little blue glow of the gas-jet under the saucepan bubbling gently on the stove.

5

I passed many evenings thus, alone in the room, waiting for Cilia, pacing up and down or lying on the bed, absorbed in that silent emptiness as the dusk slowly deepened into dark. Subdued or distant noises – the shouts of children, the bustle of the street, the cries of birds – reached me only faintly. Cilia soon realised that I didn't want to be bothered with her when I came home, and she would put her head out of Amalia's room, still sewing, to hear me pass and call to me. I didn't care whether she heard me or not, but if she did I would say something or other. Once I asked Amalia, quite seriously, why she didn't come up to our room any more, where there was plenty of light. Amalia said nothing; Cilia looked away and her face grew red.

One night, for something to say, I told her about Malagigi and made her laugh gaily at that funny little man. Then I added: ' Fancy him making a fortune and going to China! I wish it had been me!'

' I should like it, too,' Cilia sighed, ' if we went to China.'

I gave a wry grin. ' In a photograph, perhaps, if we sent one to Malagigi.'

' Why not one for ourselves?' she said. ' Oh, George, we haven't ever had a photograph of us together.'

' No money.'

' Do let's have a photograph.'

'But we oughtn't to afford it. We're together day and night, and anyway I don't like photographs.'

'We are married and we have no record of it. Let's have just one!'

I did not reply.

'It wouldn't cost much. I'll pay for it.'

'Get it done with Amalia.'

Next morning Cilia lay with her face to the wall, her hair over her eyes. She would not take any notice of me, or even look at me. I caressed her a little, then realised she was resisting me, so I jumped out of bed in a rage. Cilia got up, too, washed her face and gave me some coffee, her manner quiet and cautious, her eyes downcast. I went away without speaking to her.

An hour later I came back again. 'How much is there in the savings book?' I shouted. Cilia looked at me in surprise. She was sitting on the stool, unhappy and bewildered.

'I don't know. You've got it. About 300 *lire*, I think.'

Nearly three hundred and sixteen. Here it is,' I flung the roll of notes on the table. 'Spend it as you like. Let's have a high old time! It's all yours.'

Cilia stood up and came over to face me. 'Why have you done this, George?'

'Because I'm a fool. Listen! I'd rather not talk about it. When money is in your pocket it doesn't count any more. D'you still want that photograph?'

'But, George, I want you to be happy.'

'I am happy.'

'I do love you so much.'

'I love you, too.' I took her by the arm, sat down, and pulled her on my knee. 'Put your head here, on my shoulder.' My voice was indulgent and intimate. Cilia said nothing and leaned her cheek against mine. 'When shall we go?' I asked.

'It doesn't matter,' she whispered.

'Then listen!' I held the back of her neck and smiled at
her. Cilia, still trembling, threw her arms around my
shoulders and tried to kiss me.

'Darling!' I said. 'Let's make plans. We have three
hundred *lire*. Let's drop everything and go on a little trip.
Quickly! Now! If we think it over we'll change our minds.
Don't tell anyone about it, not even Amalia. We'll only be
away a day. It will be the honeymoon we didn't have.'

'George, why wouldn't you take me away then? You
said it was a silly idea, then.'

'Yes, but this isn't a honeymoon. You see, now we know
each other. We're good friends. Nobody knows we're going.
And, besides, we need a holiday. Don't you?'

'Of course, George. I'm so happy. Where shall we go?'

'I don't know, but we'll go at once. Would you like us
to go to the sea? To Genoa?'

6

Once we were on the train, I showed a certain preoccupation. As we started, Cilia was almost beside herself with
delight, held my hand and tried to make me talk. Then,
finding me moody and unresponsive, she quickly understood and settled down quietly, looking out of the window
with a happy smile. I remained silent, staring into nothing-
ness, listening to the rhythmic throb of the wheels on the
rails as it vibrated through my whole body. There were
other people in the carriage, but I scarcely noticed them.
Fields and hills were flashing past. Cilia, sitting opposite
and leaning on the window-pane, seemed to be listening to
something, too, but now and then she glanced swiftly in

my direction and tried to smile. So she spied on me, at a distance.

When we arrived it was dark, and at last we found somewhere to stay, in a large, silent hotel, hidden among the trees of a deserted avenue, after going up and down an eternity of tortuous streets, making enquiries. It was a grey, cold night, that made me want to stride along with my nose in the air. Instead, Cilia, tired to death, was dragging on my arm and I was only too glad to find somewhere to sit down. We had wandered through so many brightly-lit streets, so many dark alleys that brought our hearts into our mouths, but we had never reached the sea. No-one took any notice of us. We looked like any couple out for a stroll, except for our tendency to step off the pavements, and Cilia's anxious glances at the houses and passers-by.

That hotel would do for us: nothing elegant about it. A bony young fellow with his sleeves rolled up was eating at a white table. We were received by a tall, fierce-looking woman wearing a coral necklace. I was glad to sit down. Walking with Cilia never left me free to absorb myself in what I saw, or in myself. Pre-occupied and ill-at-ease, I nevertheless had to keep her beside me and answer her, at least with gestures. Now, all I wanted – and how I wanted it – was to look around and get to know in my heart of hearts this unknown city. That was precisely why I had come.

We waited downstairs to order supper, without even going upstairs to see our room or discussing terms. I was attracted by that young fellow with his auburn whiskers and his vague, lonely manner. On his forearm was a faded tattoo mark, and as he went away he picked up a patched blue jacket.

It was midnight when we had our supper. At our little

table, Cilia laughed a great deal at the disdainful air of the landlady. ' She thinks we're only just married,' she faltered. Then, her weary eyes full of tenderness, she asked me: ' And are we really?' as she stroked my hand.

We enquired about places in the neighbourhood. The harbour was only a hundred yards away, at the end of the avenue. ' Let's go and see it for a minute,' said Cilia. She was fit to drop, but she wanted to take that little walk with me.

We came to the railings of a terrace and caught our breath. The night was calm but dark, and the street-lamps floundered in the cold black abyss that lay before us. I said nothing, and my heart leapt as I breathed the smell of it, wild and free. Cilia looked around her and pointed out to me a line of lights, their reflection quivering in the water. Was it a ship? A breakwater? We could hear waves splashing gently in the darkness. ' Tomorrow,' she breathed ecstatically, ' Tomorrow we'll see it all.'

As we made our way back to our hotel, Cilia clung tightly to my side. ' How tired I am! George, it's lovely! Tomorrow! I'm so happy! Are you happy, too?' and she rubbed her cheek against my shoulder.

I did not feel like that. I was walking with clenched jaws, taking deep breaths and letting the wind caress me. I felt restless, remote from Cilia, alone in the world. Halfway up the stairs I said to her: ' I don't want to go to bed yet. You go on up. I'll go for another little stroll and come back.'

7

That time, too, it was the same. How I hurt Cilia! Even now, when I think of her in bed as dawn is breaking, I am filled with a desolate remorse for the way I treated her.

Yet I couldn't help it! I alway did everything like a fool, a man in a dream, and I did not realise the sort of man I was until the end, when even remorse was useless. Now I can glimpse the truth. I become so engrossed in solitude that it deadens all my sense of human relationships and makes me incapable of tolerating or responding to any tenderness. Cilia, for me, was not an obstacle: she simply did not exist. If I had only understood this! If I had had any idea of how much harm I was doing to myself by cutting myself off from her in this way, I should have turned to her with intense gratitude and cherished her presence as my only salvation.

But is the sight of another's suffering ever enough to open a man's eyes? Instead, it takes the sweat of agony, the bitter pain that comes as we awake, lives with us as we walk the streets, lies beside us through sleepless nights, always raw and pitiless, covering us with shame.

Dawn broke wet and cloudy. The avenue was still deserted as I wandered back to the hotel. I saw Cilia and the landlady quarrelling on the stairs, both in their night clothes. Cilia was crying. The landlady, in a dressing-gown gave a shriek as I went in. Cilia stood motionless, leaning on the handrail. Her face was white with shock, her hair and her clothes in wild disorder.

' Here he is!'

' Whatever's going on here, at this time in the morning?' I asked harshly.

The landlady, clutching her bosom, started shouting that she had been disturbed in the middle of the night because of a missing husband; there had been tears, handkerchiefs ripped to shreds, telephone calls, police enquiries. Was that the way to behave? Where did I come from?

I was so weary I could hardly stand. I gave her a listless glance of disgust. Cilia had not moved. She stood there breathing deeply through her open mouth, her face red and distorted. ' Cilia,' I cried, ' haven't you been to sleep?'

She still did not reply. She just stood there, motionless, making no attempt to wipe away the tears that streamed from her eyes. Her hands were clasped at her waist, tearing at her handkerchief.

' I went for a walk,' I said in a hollow voice. ' I stopped by the harbour.' The landlady seemed about to interrupt me, then shrugged her shoulders. ' Anyway, I'm alive, and dying for the want of sleep. Let me throw myself on the bed.'

I slept until two, heavily as a drunkard, then I awoke with a start. The light in the room was dim, but I could hear noises in the street. Instinctively I did not move. Cilia was there, sitting in a corner, looking at me, staring at the walls, examining her fingers, jumping up now and then. After a while I whispered cautiously: ' Cilia, are you watching me?' Swiftly she raised her eyes. The shattered look I had seen earlier now seemed engraved on her face. She moved her lips to speak, but no sound came.

' Cilia, a husband shouldn't be watched,' I said in a playful voice like a child's. ' Have you had anything to eat today?' The poor girl shook her head. I jumped out of bed and looked at the clock. ' The train goes at half past three,' I cried. ' Come on, Cilia, hurry! Let's try to look happy in front of the landlady.' She did not move, so I went over and pulled her up by her cheeks.

' Listen,' I went on. ' Is it because of last night?' Her eyes filled with tears. ' I could have lied, said I had got lost, smoothed things over. I didn't do that, because I hate lies. Cheer up! I have always liked to be alone. Still, even I,' and I felt her give a start, ' even I haven't enjoyed myself much at Genoa. Yet I'm not crying.'

24th November – 6th December, 1936

Summer Storm

The sun had not yet reached the bathing-hut on the landing-stage at the foot of the hills. Great trees overshadowed it. The river gleamed an even white in the dawn, and on the far bank houses in scattered suburbs began to show lights. Over there it seemed broad daylight already. The old boat-woman, dirty and dishevelled, was going along the line of punts moored to the landing-stage, pulling them in, one by one, then bending forward with her left hand on her hip to haul in the slack ropes. Every time a boat wedged itself between two others, the bump was passed along the whole line, setting them all rocking in the current.

A hessian curtain hung across the back of the hut and from behind it came sounds of movements and voices. Somebody was undressing.

'Look at this silk blouse! Is it yours?' a harsh voice cried. 'And these silk stockings?'

The old woman looked up crossly, stopping her work. The reflection from a few pink clouds above the trees shone on the river and cast a glow over her face.

'Here's a skirt, too,' the voice went on. 'Lovely quality! And another one!'

The curtain was pulled aside and a young fellow came out, buttoning the shoulder of his swimming costume. He was short and not very muscular, but sunburnt and curly haired.

'And we meant to be first, this time! Gosh! It's cold, here,' he said, slapping his thighs, all pimply with goose-flesh, and jumping up and down. 'We talked about making it a foursome if we could get a couple of girls out of bed this early and take them boating.'

'There's a couple of girls ahead of you, all by themselves,' the old woman told him, bending to her work again. 'Alone and full of beans. Since no one was here to see them they didn't mind waking people up before it was light. They didn't even give me time to comb my hair. Women!'

'Alone!' the young fellow cried as he jumped about. 'D'you hear that, Moro? Two girls on their own ahead of us! Come on out of there!' He turned and asked the old woman: 'What are they like? What sort are they?'

'Haven't you just seen their clothes?' she answered with a grin. 'From a woman's slip to her skin is no great distance.'

'That's nothing to go by. Who are they?'

'They aren't regular customers. One is thin, her hair and skin as pale as straw. The other hadn't much to say but she's already tanned dark brown by the sun, well-built and so full of energy that she almost capsized the boat when she jumped in. Both of them were very stuck-up and stand-offish.'

'Have they been gone long?'

'An hour or so.'

'Pretty? What colour bathing costumes?'

'Ask her if they took their handbags with them, Aurelio,' the first voice called sharply from behind the curtain.

'That friend of yours sounds a bright lad,' the old woman chuckled with a wink. Raising her voice she added: 'Don't worry. They can pay for their own boat. They look as if they're worth much more than that.'

'Depends who they come across,' and the second man emerged from behind the curtain, a tall, bony fellow with great sweaty feet and red hands, fastening his baggy swim-suit over shoulders as pale as the belly of a fish. He looked straight at the old woman, whose face still twinkled with mischief, and a flash of ill-temper gleamed in his eyes.

She looked him up and down stealthily and remarked: 'So we're new here, are we? Never been out in a boat all this year, by what I can see.'

Aurelio broke in: 'He looks a lot better with an oar in his hand. Then he'd beat all those family men you've tipped into the Po. Any oar! Even a bit of wood!'

'I've never seen him rowing past here though. By the look of him, I'd say the poor soul was at his last gasp after three months of sciatica. Glad to get a bit of fresh air again, eh?'

The young man screwed up his mouth and spat on the ground. Without turning round he asked his companion, out of the corner of his mouth, 'Got everything?'

Aurelio slipped behind the curtain and brought out a small case that he put into the first punt. Then he jumped aboard and stood with his legs wide apart, rocking the little boat to work it free of the others and creating tumultuous repercussions all along the line.

'It's quite ready,' the old woman cried, bringing along a paddle and a punt pole with an iron rim. 'I baled out just now, after those other two got me out of bed. All you've got to do is get in,' and with a powerful sweep of her arm she swung out the heavy pole.

'Let's hope so,' Aurelio replied.

The old woman turned with a grin to Moro, who was standing there doing nothing, and eyed him again, curiously, from head to foot. To Aurelio she said: 'Your friend still looks bleary-eyed. Watch out! If you run into a bridge there'll be damages to pay.'

'You be careful nobody runs into you,' Moro retorted. He clambered awkwardly into the boat, making Aurelio nearly lose his balance. 'Hand over that paddle,' he said coldly as he turned round, 'and cast off.'

The old woman did as he told her. Aurelio looked up at the sky. By now the pink clouds had gone. Standing in the stern, Aurelio thrust the pole straight down and forced the boat out with all the power of his wrists from among the others until it swung free as the current caught it. 'Cheerio,' the old woman muttered, but neither man made any reply and she went back to the bathing-hut.

Aurelio, in his black swimsuit, kept raising and lowering the pole, probing the bottom, bending forward to exert his utmost strength against the pressure of the water. He looked steadily ahead at the smooth, shining stream, screwing up his eyes against the glare. He came out into the sunlight.

Moro was lying in the bottom of the boat, filling it completely, his hairy legs dangling over the sides. He raised his hand to shade his eyes.

'Isn't the sunshine grand, Moro?'

'It's grand to see it from here,' Moro muttered.

'It's the same everywhere,' Aurelio replied. 'But it won't be so bright for long, this morning. Look at those clouds coming up.'

'The worst of it is, when you're inside, all the sun does is heat your cell. It's not just sunshine, it's a blazing furnace.'

'Then in winter it keeps you warm.'

'In winter you freeze and you can't say a thing. But the worst thing is that in summer, when there's a sun like this, you've got to stick it out in jacket and trousers. Take your jacket off? No, sir, not on your life! Take off your jacket when they let you out in the exercise yard? You can't. Why not? You just can't.'

'It's the same for soldiers, anyway.'

'No, this was worse. They shut a man up just so as to make him walk round the dustbins.'

Aurelio, bending forward to thrust in the pole, laughed down into Moro's face. Moro, raising his hand and screwing up his eyes, grinned back at him.

Covering his eyes again, Moro went on : 'Once a man's in prison it means he's a bad lot. Nobody wants no-goods like us. They tell us we must change our way of life and meantime they keep us shut up like rabbits. If we're to change our way of living they should let us get on with it, turn us loose at once. Instead, no. You've got to stay there two, three, ten years, depending on what your record says; turn yellow, green, grey – that's the only change in life you'll get. D'you know that where I was there was a man serving twenty years? He looked like my grandfather did when he was dead, yet he was only forty. Murder. All because he'd had a drop too much.'

'Still, some fools let themselves be caught when they shouldn't,' said Aurelio as he bent forward again.

Moro started up to sit facing Aurelio. 'But what if justice is worse than we are?' he exclaimed. 'Why don't they kill a man right off if they catch him at it? Or, if he's just picking pockets, give him a sound thrashing, like men? Then we'd soon see who had the best of it. It's a priests' trick to keep a man shut up for years. Don't you think so?'

'But all they gave you was a year and a half.'

'A year's nothing. It's the days that are so long.'

'You didn't used to be so dim, Moro. You haven't got the prison food out of your system, yet. It's upset your stomach and you look scared stiff.'

Moro rummaged in the attaché-case and brought out a cigarette. The pale little flame in the sunshine showed up the pale little hollows in his drawn cheeks. He tossed the match away.

Aurelio said : 'What you ought to be doing is learning
a bit more sense. Take care where you operate another
time. Who ever heard of a stick-up in broad daylight?
You're no good at that sort of job, anyway.'

'I'm all right in a boat, though,' Moro exclaimed, jumping to his feet so suddenly that Aurelio almost overbalanced.
'Give me that pole.'

Cautiously Aurelio edged over to Moro's side and passed
him the pole. Then he sat down and tried to smoke. Moro,
his cigarette twisted between his lips, felt for the bottom
and made his first thrust, then slowly straightened up.

Bianca raised her dripping paddle and the punt glided
forward under the trees into the still water. 'The sunshine's
gone,' Clara grumbled.

Bianca, clenching her teeth, threw herself down on the
bank and looked around. 'It's that cloud making the water
seem dark,' she said. 'If the sun comes out again it will be
all silvery.'

'Is it going to rain?'

'I don't think so, but even if it does, we're here to go
swimming.'

'You're a real river-girl,' Clara murmured, and Bianca
looked away, determined not to lose her temper at the
lazy mockery in her friend's eyes.

Clara remarked : 'Why ever didn't you notice how low
the swallows are flying over the Po?'

Bianca swung round to look at the river. Through the
little opening where they had come in she could see the
current running swiftly past in a belt of sunlight. Out in
mid-stream a dredger was floating, moored to a slanting
cable and rocking as the water rippled round it. It was quite
deserted.

'That's where we can go if it rains. I've never been on board a dredger.'

'There isn't a soul about,' Clara said. 'Once those poor sand-grubbers have gone home – and seeing they spend their life on the water they could at least wash themselves – the river is a desert. Anyone could die – or be born – here and nobody would know. It's like some bygone civilization.' She leaned over the side of the boat and added: 'Except for all those sardine tins and broken jars. They strike a different note. Actually I don't think much of your river.'

Clara's supple body in its tight-fitting yellow bathing costume threw back a pale reflection as she leaned over the greenish water. Bianca watched her almost against her will, making no reply. But then she smiled. Clara was gazing at her own face in the water and rubbing the corner of her eye with one finger. 'So any mirror's enough to put the fair lady Clara in a better humour,' Bianca mocked, conscious that her voice was shaking uncontrollably.

'Taking one mirror with another, I prefer my own. At least in that one I don't see a shoal of little fish shooting out of my mouth. and it doesn't make me look drunk. Nor does it give me a halo from a sunken bowl.'

Involuntarily, Bianca's fists clenched, but she controlled herself, stretching out her arms and relaxing her cramped fingers. At ease again, she turned her head, letting her eyes wander over the sky and the trees on the bank. Beyond their trunks stretched a pleasant beach, shining against a mass of cloud. 'I didn't promise you the River Amazon,' she said good-humouredly, 'but that's what we'll get if it rains. Why take shelter, anyway? What can be lovelier than a morning storm?'

'Listen, dear. If you want to have a swim, get on with it. It's going to pour any minute and my costume isn't meant to get wet.'

'I want to see you get in.'

170

'Bianca! Is that why you've brought me all up here? For me to jump into that black water and get covered with filthy mud and bitten by crocodiles? Bianca! I have pretty skin and it needs looking after. It's a good thing that sun you're so fond of has been kind and respectful to a poor blonde without much on.'

'Stupid,' Bianca replied with a shrug. 'This life would do you good, make you stronger and more confident.'

'But I'm strong already. Too strong and self-reliant, really. What I need is the opposite. It's cost me one love affair, being so strong.'

Bianca bent down to undo her canvas shoes, looking sideways at Clara and listening as she went on : 'It never does to show people you're strong and self-reliant. They're only too ready to knock it out of you.'

'Why don't you give up this aimless way of life?' Bianca asked with a smile.

'It isn't as dull as some, you know.'

'I see,' Bianca murmured softly, feeling in her bag for her rubber bathing-cap.

When she stood ready she turned to Clara, who lay at full length in the bottom of the boat grinning up at her. 'So you really aren't coming?' she asked.

'You go, and come back in triumph. I'll give you a clap.'

'Won't you at least swim in here? I'll hold you up.'

'My precious, you're too silly for words. One plays that game with men, not with another girl. Off you go, and don't break your neck.'

Bianca shivered as she entered the water, and waded with uncertain steps towards the opening. Then she clenched her teeth and dived. The water was not cold. Over here in mid-stream the dredger was twinkling in the sun. She stood up again with the water up to her waist, and felt the wind cold on her shoulders.

She passed the ripples swirling by the opening and saw the current running strongly ahead. The bottom was deeper now. She glanced over her shoulder at the surface of the water, the low banks, the boat, the vague blur of trees, then stretched herself in a powerful swimming stroke. Suddenly she was out into the tumbling current. She turned up-stream from the dredger, swimming straight towards the hill now veiled by the sun and clouds, and plunging her face into the dark gurgling water, catching her breath as best she could in the pauses between her arm strokes. Her progress across the current threatened to break her rhythm at any moment and she could see nothing but flashing drops of spray. Exhausted by her efforts to breathe she dropped her head for the last time and suddenly saw the water below the surface made transparent by diffused sunlight. She raised her head. The dredger was only a few yards away.

Bianca worked her way around the rocking hull, looking for somewhere to hold on. A shadow ran across the water. The last of the sunshine had gone. The chill wind blew stronger.

Bianca pulled herself up, scraping her knee on the vessel's side. The metal superstructure with its pulleys and sand-encrusted gratings took up most of the space, leaving only a narrow ledge all round. Unsteadily she made her way along it and came to a hut of rough boards tucked in among the machinery. It had an earthy floor and a pile of folded sacks in one corner. In the middle, the deck was cut away, leaving an empty space of bubbling black water – the river itself. A chain of buckets hung down into it from an opening dimly visible in the roof high above.

Bianca went outside again to watch the current rushing out from below the hull, and her eyes opened in wide amazement at the flood pouring down towards the weir, broken by stones and torn branches. She reflected that only an hour earlier they had been punting on the river, and she remembered Clara.

She ran to the side of the dredger and looked for the little break in the woods where they had landed. At first she saw nothing but the low, green bank, distant and motionless under the swaying trees. Then, behind a spit of land, she caught sight of Clara's light-coloured costume. She was standing waving the paddle, shouting shrilly and pointing at the sky.

'There's shelter here,' Bianca yelled. 'It's safe enough.'

Apparently Clara heard, for she waved her hand and disappeared behind the little promontory. The first thunder rumbled in the distance. Nervously, Bianca whipped off her rubber cap. Terrifying clouds were piling up, and a sudden bright flash of lightning darted across the sky. Bianca pressed her hands on the hull and stared down at the water swirling and foaming below her. The thunder did not come for a moment and she started shouting: 'Clara it's . . .'

There came a low roar that gradually grew louder and louder, echoing among the hills and swelling like the noise of a landslide until it crashed in the distance and died away with a dull reverberation. Bianca flushed as her fears left her. It was raining in the city, for certain. Down there in the valley the sky looked terrible.

'Clara, it's all right here. I'm coming to fetch you.' Cold wind-squalls blowing up the river whistled round the dredger, making it swing on its mooring. 'Where on earth has she got to, the silly girl!' Bianca muttered to herself, peering at the low bank and the tall trees swaying wildly against the clear streak of the horizon.

Then she saw the boat coming out of the opening with Clara in it, frenziedly straining with the paddle and raising great splashes of foam. But once out in the current she lost course, caught up in the eddies and gusts of wind.

'Careful!' Bianca yelled. 'You'll end up over the weir!'

173

and she ran along the hull, watching the boat being swept inexorably downstream. Then Clara stood up. (The thought flashed into Bianca's mind that she looked just like a canary.) She seized the heavy, iron-rimmed pole and leaned forward to thrust it in over the stern. The punt swung further downstream. Clara was gripping the pole with all her might, holding it upright and trying to find the bottom. There was no bottom, and every time she tried to probe for it the current drove the punt hard against the pole, wrenching her wrists painfully. 'Idiot!' Bianca howled, almost beside herself. 'Go sideways! Put that pole down. Use the paddle!'

She was frantically pulling on her cap again when she heard a scream. Clara had disappeared. She had fallen into the water behind the punt. A patch of wild splashing in the wake of the boat showed where she was struggling.

Bianca dived in, at the same moment almost blinded by a lightning flash. Only in the water could she feel safe. She swam desperately, head down, seeing nothing, hearing nothing, not even the thunder clap. For the moment she was not thinking of Clara. She was straining every nerve to reach the punt and salvage the pole. Then she could save Clara.

Her arm bumped against the pole. Looking round through the spray, she could see something yellow splashing about some distance away; in the other direction, in the grip of the current, she saw the empty punt. 'Without the boat I'll never manage to pull her out' flashed through her mind, and pushing the pole ahead of her she made for the punt. She reached it and threw in the pole. Heaving herself over the side, out of the rushing water, almost tore her shoulders apart, but at last she rolled in, bruised all over and seized the paddle. When she turned round there was no longer any sign of Clara. Only then did she notice it was raining in torrents, great blasts that cut furrows in the surface of the river. Clouds of fine spray like smoke billowed everywhere and her back began to tingle, stung by the violence of the downpour.

Clara was no longer there. Bianca tossed her head to free her eyes from the matted hair that was blinding her. She had lost her cap, and had to run her fingers through her hair before she could push it away. A wild yell burst from her: 'Clara!'

All around her the water boiled, its surface unbroken. Steering the boat with the paddle and holding it steady against the current she peered into the swirling flood, trying to find the place where Clara had disappeared. Millions of tiny bubbles spread a layer of pale foam between the water and the air. Through the raindrops Bianca looked for the bank, but everything had vanished. All she could see was a vague outline. She was alone on the river.

Plying the paddle frenziedly she made some headway against the current, thankful to be still afloat, heedless of her direction. Then, through the hair still hanging over her eyes, she noticed she was level with a certain tall tree growing on the bank. Her teeth chattering with fright, she jumped to her feet in the drenching rain and put down the paddle. 'She called me a "river girl",' she murmured breathlessly and plunged in, hurting her foot badly.

Under the surface she found a great calm. The dense mass of water deadened every sound, made every effort seem remote and pointless. She strained her eyes in the darkness and groped about with her hands, but she saw nothing and felt nothing except the weight of the water. When she surfaced she was surprised by the light and the rain. She had quite forgotten them. The punt was not far away. She turned and dived again, probing about until her ears were buzzing and her arm-strokes grew weak. She surfaced again and swam to the boat, clinging to it with her whole body and tearing her costume as she clambered in.

Ankle-deep in water, she picked up the paddle again and looked around her, uncertain what to do. Then her heart leapt. There in the mist was another boat with two men in it, creeping along the opposite bank and making straight for the dredger.

Bianca jumped to her feet and started shouting, waving the paddle. The warm rain splashed into her mouth. The men did not turn. 'Over here!' she yelled, loud enough to split her throat. She almost added: 'Help!', but refrained. Her bag was floating in the bottom of the punt. She pulled out a towel and waved it, still shouting.

The men were now level with the dredger and paddled round, looking up at it. As Bianca watched, one of them jumped aboard it and the other, bending forward in the rain, handed up a rope. She glanced at the foaming current as it swept past, loaded with mud, then, clenching her teeth, she turned the boat towards the dredger and paddled furiously.

Out of the rain her half-drowned head came level with the hull. 'Oh!' Aurelio was saying as he threw himself down on the sacks, 'Look at the state we're in!' Moro, standing naked at the back of the hut, wringing out his swimming trunks, did not turn.

'Here's a woman!' Aurelio exclaimed.

She clutched the rail with both hands and the little boat slid from under her feet. 'A girl's been drowned,' she cried shrilly. 'Come and help me.'

Aurelio ran forward to give her a hand. 'If you don't come aboard, you'll be drowned, too,' he cried. 'Moro, come and help!'

The girl, her hand in Aurelio's, looked back and forth from him to the river. She was steaming like a horse; her sunburnt skin looked sodden and lifeless; her arms and legs were covered with scratches.

'A friend of mine's been drowned,' she cried. 'I've got to find her. I've been calling for ages.'

'Even the fishes would drown on a day like this,' said Moro in the darkness of the hut, holding his trunks to shield his hairy stomach.

'Jump in! Jump in,' Aurelio urged again. 'You're over the worst. If it was all that time ago, she's dead by now. Where did it happen?'

'Down there,' the girl sobbed, pointing to the current and trying to release her other hand. 'Over there.'

'She went under?'

'D'you expect people to drown in the air?' Moro sneered in the background.

'Jump in,' said Aurelio. 'Too much water is bad for anyone. There's a hut here. Your boat's waterlogged already.'

Moro came forward with his costume draped around him. 'Where does she say it happened?' he asked.

'Over there. Just beyond the Sangone.' She turned her eyes in that direction and the drops fell from her matted hair like a flood of tears.

'Come on into shelter,' Aurelio persisted, pulling her by the arm. 'If that's where she went down, the current won't carry her beyond the weir. We know where to find her. Was she the same age as you?'

'Could she swim?' Moro added.

'Can you swim yourself?' the girl asked sharply.

Moro flung himself down on a seat at the edge of the hut, his trunks between his thighs. Aurelio was still bending over the side trying to pull the girl in, and Moro kicked him on the ankle. 'Don't you see?' he said out of the corner of his mouth. 'These are the girls from the landing-stage. My dear bathing beauty,' he went on, 'we can swim

177

a lot better than people like you who come here to act the fool when other folk are working, but we swim in water, not in rain. We'll see about that later, if you like. But for the present, we'll let it rain. Leave her to get out of it by herself.'

Aurelio, uncertain what to do, relaxed his hold and went back into the hut, the water dripping from him. Slowly the boat drifted backwards. The girl stood there for a moment, raising her shoulder to rub her cheek. Then she leaned forward, picked up the paddle and brought the punt alongside the dredger again.

Without a word she pulled herself up on the hull, holding the boat's mooring chain between her teeth. Then she turned her back and crouched forward to thread the chain through a ring in the hull. As she did so, she found that her black costume was split all down the left side and torn at the hem on her thigh. Her white flesh gleamed through the holes, very different from the bronzed skin of her legs and shoulders.

Having secured the chain, she leaned forward to take her bag from the boat. Aurelio's eyes followed the play of her pale skin under her torn costume. Without looking at him, the girl staggered to her feet – she was short and dark, like him – and put down her sodden bag inside the hut. Then she sat down under the shelter, apart from the other two, her knees against her chest. She rested her elbows on them and took her cheeks in her hands, sitting very still and staring at the rain.

The whole dredger quivered and rocked as the current washed past it. Down from the opening in the roof of the hut where the pulley-chains ran came cold blasts that cut into their backs. Aurelio, crouching on his sacks, looked at Moro's long, bare spine and the girl's shoulders, shining against the background of the rain.

'Moro,' he said suddenly, breaking the silence, 'cover

up your seat, or this draught'll give you a chill.'

Moro grinned across at him. 'It's not proper to put on one's trousers in the presence of a young lady.'

'D'you think you're so handsome? Young ladies don't look.'

'They're too well brought up to say anything.'

Aurelio stuffed one hand into the little case lying on the sacks. 'Want a cigarette?'

'If they're not soaked, too.'

Aurelia stood up and held out the packet to Moro, taking one out with his lips at the same time. Then he turned to the girl and offered her one. 'Let's have a smoke on it,' he said. She made no response but still sat motionless, staring at the rain.

'Thanks very much, but I don't smoke,' he prompted her as he went back to the sacks and struck a match.

'You see what women are like,' Moro told him, trying in vain to strike a match in his turn. 'The whole world at their beck and call. Acting so foolhardy and running into danger when they haven't any idea what the Po can be like. When a man reasons with them they spit at his feet and ask him if he can swim. Somebody who can really swim doesn't let anyone drown. What'll you bet, Aurelio, that the other girl couldn't swim, either?'

Irritably, Aurelio threw away his cigarette and wandered restlessly round the hut, trying out the chain that held the buckets. He thrust his hand inside his costume to rub his shivering chest and finally came to sit beside the girl at the front of the hut. Moro was watching her out of the corner of his eye. Like her, Aurelio pulled his knees against his chest and rested his cheeks on his hands. 'Pretty girls don't cry,' he told her with a wink.

She flushed, jumped to her feet and turned to go inside, but Aurelio held her by the arm and tried to pull her back. Then he let her go. 'All right, all right,' he said. 'We know each other. At least I know your friend was a blonde.'

The girl stared at him a moment with blazing eyes. 'I told you myself,' she muttered as she ran inside. Then she swung round in the gloom and asked him : 'How did you manage to find out that?'

'I'll tell you, if you tell me your name,' Aurelio smiled as he rose to his feet.

'It's Piccone,' she answered quickly. 'So what?'

Moro burst out laughing and slapped his thigh.

'Your own name,' Aurelio persisted, still smiling. 'What does your surname matter to me?'

She stood still a moment, disconcerted. Then her whole face flamed red and distorted, as if he had struck her across the mouth.

Suddenly an oath burst from Moro. He had jumped up hurriedly and his trunks had fallen overboard. Dropping to his knees he stretched his arm down but failed to reach them. Then, naked as he was, he leapt into the girl's boat with a great splash and fished them out, dripping wet. He climbed up again, still uncovered. 'Blast! They were practically dry,' he exclaimed as he threw them down in a corner and stalked into the hut.

The girl watched him come, her eyes fixed on his face. Without glancing aside, he said, from the corner of his mouth : 'Both those boats are full of water. Go and bale them out, Aurelio.' The girl backed away.

'Where have we seen the blonde, Miss Piccone?' Moro sneered, his face close to hers. 'The dead float, you fool! They can swim much better than you or me. D'you know where that blonde is now?' Moro's voice sank to a chilling whisper. The girl could see his teeth. 'She's here behind you, in this patch of water. Her eyes are open and her nails all broken. She's calling you, raising her hand. She's going to grab you!'

Terrified, the girl crouched down on the sacks. Moro laughed over her shoulders. 'Silly fool,' he said, gripping her sides with his hands.

Aurelio shook him by the shoulder. 'You can't do things like that, you great lout. You're only frightening her. D'you think you're still in prison? I was the one who helped her. It's my affair.'

The girl struggled to her knees. Moro thrust her down again with his fist in her neck and his shin in the small of her back. Suddenly he turned his tense, fleshless face to Aurelio and said with a grin. 'Go and bale out those punts, I tell you. This Piccone girl has seen me; she's fallen for me; she wants me.'

'You shouldn't have got stripped. It isn't fair.'

'Sure,' Moro retorted, swaying as the girl struggled beneath him. 'I don't want any of your nonsense. Go and bale out the punts. They're sinking.'

The girl collapsed on the sacks so suddenly that Moro almost fell on top of her. Her limp body in its torn black costume lay white and slack.

'You've killed her!' Aurelio cried.

'They're like cats. They squeal if you only hold them under water.'

Out in the rain again, Aurelio stared at the current instead of seeing to the boats, watching it foaming, yellow with mud, under the water streaming from the sky. Eddies formed, swirled away and formed again round the dredger as it swung and rolled in the fierce grip of the flood, all its metal parts clanking noisily. Now and then a broken oar flashed past, glimpsed for an instant before it rolled under again. Over in the valley, everything looked vague and indistinct; the masses of trees on the deserted banks seemed in a different world. One could guess how the water must be roaring and foaming over the rapids by the weir.

Both punts were full. The one the girl had brought was

half submerged. Aurelio glanced sideways at the dripping entrance to the hut, then threw himself forward and picked up a short end of wood floating in the boat. Blinded by the rain, he leaned out from the hull and made a few aimless movements with it. Then he drew back again as heavy breathing and a long, low groan reached him from the hut, and the sound of material being ripped. He looked round quickly and glimpsed in the gloom a pale, shapeless mass of struggling bodies.

He sat down again on the hull, stretching out his brown legs in the rain and staring at the punt as it rocked gently. The water inside it was clear, compared with the river, and the varnished bottom planking shone through. The iron-rimmed pole was still there. The paddle had been washed away.

He heard Moro cursing, but would not turn round. He heard sounds of a struggle and a long moan. Then, silence except for the rain.

Aurelio unbuttoned his swim-suit at the shoulder and rolled it down to his waist. He examined his chest as he breathed in and out. The cold air tasted of mud and leaves. Then he tried to purse up his lips and whistle a tune, but no sound came out.

'Aurelio! Quick!' Moro's hoarse voice broke the silence. 'Here's another one dead!'

Aurelio sprang up. Moro was sitting at the back of the hut, clutching his knees against his chest. Aurelio barely had time to glimpse the girl lying at full length before she leapt to her feet, deathly white in spite of great black bruises, her costume in tatters. She fled across the dark space, pushed Aurelio aside and fell into the water.

Aurelio had knocked his knee against the planks but he recovered his balance and turned round as a roar of laughter from Moro made his ears ring.

'She's done it on you! See! That's women for you!'

The girl was already some way off, swimming spasmodically with great splashes, half out of the water. Aurelio jumped into the boat, almost capsizing it. It took him a moment or two to cast off.

'It's no good,' Moro said, coming up beside him. 'I told you to bale out. You won't do it now in the time. You've let her get away.'

Aurelio would have thrown himself into the water in his frenzy, but Moro held him back. 'She won't get far. A woman's worn out when I've finished with her. Watch!'

The girl was rolling helplessly in the current, incapable of guiding herself, and ending up in mid-stream, splashing feebly and drifting rapidly towards the weir. 'So she can't swim,' said Moro. 'Still, I gave her a good lesson.'

'She's drowning,' Aurelio cried, 'and I . . .'

'Come back in the shadow,' Moro urged, pulling him by the arm. 'Have you gone crazy? It couldn't be better. She left us of her own free will. Besides, girls like her always talk.'

Aurelio had lost sight of that black speck and stood trembling, straining his eyes.

'Now I'll have a smoke. Be glad to,' Moro said as he went back inside. When, a few minutes later, Aurelio joined him and threw himself down on the sacks, Moro went on curtly: 'Have a cigarette. Never mind. You shall do it first another time.'